BLACK ROSE

BLACK ROSE

KEN J

Black Rose

Copyright © 2022 by Ken J. All rights reserved.

No part of this publication may be reproduced, stored in a retrieval system or transmitted in any way by any means, electronic, mechanical, photocopy, recording or otherwise without the prior permission of the author except as provided by USA copyright law.

The opinions expressed by the author are not necessarily those of URLink Print and Media.

1603 Capitol Ave., Suite 310 Cheyenne, Wyoming USA 82001
1-888-980-6523 | admin@urlinkpublishing.com

URLink Print and Media is committed to excellence in the publishing industry.

Book design copyright © 2022 by URLink Print and Media. All rights reserved.

Published in the United States of America

Library of Congress Control Number: 2022910557
ISBN 978-1-68486-210-8 (Paperback)
ISBN 978-1-68486-211-5 (Digital)

19.05.22

INTRODUCTION

KENDRA AND KENDALL A PAIR OF INDENTICAL TWIN HIT MEN. WANTS REVENGE ON THE CRIME BOSS THAT KILLED THIER FATHER BOTH WOMEN ARE VERY GOOD AT WHAT THEY DO NOW THE HUNT IS ON.

CHAPTER 1

Curtis Sandaro was one of five kids and the oldest, having just graduated high school it was his day off of work. He went to meet his friends but he got to the spot a little early so he waited a man saw him setting on his car. The man walked up to him asking him how would you like to make on the side? Curtis ask how is that sir right now I am waiting for my friends.

The man said it is simple you would be delivering packages Curtis ask would I be able to do this around my job? The man said that can be arranged. Curtis said that sounds interesting then the man gave him a name and address where to go. Now Curtis worked at a hardware store now his friends finally showed up four of them and they all went fishing. Then coming home a little after dark with their catch cleaning them and putting them in the freezer.

The next day at work was a normal one when he got off work he went to the address given to him. After a little talk he was given a package and ask to take it to another address he did and he got paid in cash for it. He saw no harm in it so he kept it up and got paid very nicely for it. The banks back then never questioned the money going in his account, so every Friday Curtis would take his check and the cash he got from the delivery's and put them in his saving account. By the end of two years Curtis and a nice some of money saved up, with his experience He took a big chance and opened up a hardware store.

He called it Sandaro's Trading now the people he delivered for thought Curtis was on to something. One person would bring it to the store like it was a delivery someone else would go in the store like he was buying it. This would through anyone watching off soon Curtis hired one his his sisters and brother Gwen and Jake.

The store made things easier soon other people would come in to the store and talk to Curtis about other merchandise for the store and special delivery's. The special things was mixed in with their knew merchandise which would go on the shelf the special things would stay in the back. Until someone would come along and ask for it they would pay in cash at the cash register then pick it up around back.

Then one day during a delivery Curtis ask Jake to get the truck Jake said OK got it. Then went to sign off for the truck after unloading he separated the knew stuff. Finding a ball item in it calling Gwen she came back asking what is it? Jake said look at this. I think someone made a mistake Gwen said I will go ask Curtis about it she went to him saying we have a mistake delivery. He followed her Jake showed Curtis the box Curtis said someone will be in for it. Then told both of them what was going on Jake said your smuggling! Curtis said how do you think I opened this store.

Gwen ask how does it work? Curtis said we will re-box this then someone will come in asking for it with a piece of paper of the description. I will give him the box he in turn hands me and envelope with money in it, I in turn put it in the box I made under the cash register. Jake said the store is a front to move this stuff Curtis said yes these shipments do not go on the books everything else does.

The next day Curtis and Jake was in back receiving a normal shipment, Gwen was up front when two men walked in asking for Curtis. Gwen said he is busy can I help you? The two men looked at each other one said said we was wondering if you would have this in stock. Calling the item by name Gwen said we have one of those in back one man ask can you get it please? Gwen said sure be right back I will go get it. Up until now Curtis handled this Gwen ask Curtis for that item he pointed to a box she in turn took it to the men. Who in turn gave her and envelope and left she put it in the box under the counter.

When Curtis and Jake was done they came up front Curtis ask about the item Gwen said they took it and I put the envelope in here pointing to the box. Gwen ask what was in the envelope? Curtis said five thousand dollars just for that item. Gwen and Jake looked at each other they were shocked Curtis went on to say the cash bonus I give you two comes from that. Jake ask that what they pay Curtis said some will pay more near the end of the day Gwen and Jake would restore the shelves and Curtis would take the money to the bank.

Now Curtis did have a girlfriend her name was cinder Meadows her father worked on cars her mother was a waitress. They have been dating sense the eleventh grade now it has been a few years. There wedding would be three years sense they started dating Cinder had job her mother and grandmother had been sewing her wedding dress.

Cinder's wedding dress was close on being done, the chapel had been reserved and both bride and groom was nervous. Curtis went to buy a suit up until now he had never owned one, he was also coming with some money. His store was taking off along with the smuggling he only used the profits from the store while tucking away the money from the other. This way no one knew how much money Curtis really had he also used some of it to help his family out they thought it was profit from the store.

Near the end of each day Curtis would get all the money together made at the store. Then get then money from the smuggling put it together then deposit it all in his bank account. The bank never said a thing they knew he had a store, back in these days bank never question money being deposited. Curtis also kept track of everything being sold well not everything, then one day a man came in. Gwen was at the the front counter Curtis was in back Jake was cleaning, the man pulled a gun. Asking for all the money Jake heard it then grabbed the mop handle he did not see Jake. He saw Gwen try to stall when she gave him the bag Jake smacked him in back of the head.

Gwen run for Curtis Jake called the police nothing was touched until the police got there. They arrested the man on armed robbery but the story of the attempted robbery soon spread to his special clients. They got asking if thing were OK Curtis told them how it went down they smiled on how handled it. One of his clients took a gun from his pocket laid it on the counter then said here is something to help protect the store.

Gwen was behind the counter she did not know what to think Jake said with a smile mop handles come in handy. The gentleman smile saying yes indeed then left and things got busy Gwen said I don't know about having a gun in the store, Curtis said I have a feeling thing might pick up.

The store was opened six days a week closed on Sundays, but the day of his wedding he hung a sign that read close getting married. The chapel was full of his family and friends Curtis's parents gave the reception at their house. Curtis had bought a house a year before a three bedroom built in 1885 with two acres. It was after he got married a business man moved into town forty miles away from Sandaro's Trading. Through source's he found out about Curtis's store then went through these people. To have jewelry shipped like always boxed in other products with a paper describing it.

The next day after they got it one of Curtis's regular clients called telling him he was just in a car accident. He did not know when he could pick up his package Curtis said Mr. Thawson if it is good with you I can have one of my brothers deliver it to you. Thawson said I forgot you once did that, that would be find then no sooner did he hang up did his brother Charles walked in. now he had a job washes dishes he came by to get a few things for their father. Curtis ask what brings you in? Charles said dad ask me to stop by and get him a few things.

Curtis ask anything after that? Charles said no Curtis said I will pay you to deliver a package for me. This caught Charles's interest he said let me get these things to dad then I will come back. After dropping them off at his father's house he returned to the store Curtis handed him a package then said take it to this address they will pay you for it. He went to the address then knocked on the door a woman answered it saying hello may I help you? Charles said I am from Sandaro's Trading I have a package.

The woman said just a minute I will get my husband the door opened again this time it was a man. He said hello sir I hear you have a package Charles said yes sir right here, the man took the package then handed Charles a thick envelope. Returning to the store he handed it over to Curtis, Curtis in return open it up giving him five time more then what he made washing dishes. Charles looked shocked asking are you nuts? Curtis smiled saying there is more of that if you want to deliver for me. Charles ask didn't you do deliver at one time? Curtis said yes before a I open this store.

Ed Willowbrock had been in his house with his wife and daughter seven months when he began business with Sandaro's Trading. Ed called the store asking for the Jewelry Jake was talking to Ed Curtis was helping unload a truck. Jake said yes we do Ed said I an tied up with business is there any way you can bring it out to me? Jake said sure what is your address? Ed gave it to him. As Jake wrote it down after hanging up he went and told Curtis it Was Charles day off from work he was hanging the store. Curtis ask Charles want to make another delivery? Charles smiled saying sure Curtis gave him the package and the address.

It took Charles some time to find the address but he found it. Knocking on the door and asking for Ed Willowbrock, Ed took the package then gave him and envelope. Then driving back and giving Curtis the envelope in turn Curtis paid him. When open Curtis open the envelope he found just paper he said what the hell is this Gwen ask something wrong? Curtis said yes he stiff me. Charles said that is what he gave me Curtis said this is not your fault I will go talk to him tonight.

It was business like usual but after everyone went home Curtis got a pop bottle fill it full of gas. Then shoved a piece of cloth inside the top making sure some stayed out Curtis drove out their stopped

Black Rose

and got a bit to eat. Then visited some friends it got late Curtis said I need to go going and let you go to bed. He left going to Ed's house everyone was sleeping by now he lit the wick throwing it at the house slowly driving away before turning on his lights.

A neighbor got up to use the bathroom when they saw the fire, they quickly called the fire department. The smoke woke Ed he woke his wife then ran for his daughter as their house was on fire Getting out just when the fire trucks got there. The house was a lose a neighbor invited the in for the night the next morning they went through salvaged what they could. Then they went to stay with some friends until the insurance came through, when that finally came through he bought another house.

Ed drove to Sandaro's Trading now one of Curtis's special clients had just come in the store. Jake ask if he could help them? Nick was his name his wife was Minnie Nick said my wife is wanting to look around. Five minutes later Ed walked in asking Jake if he was the owner? Jake called Curtis saying he is. Curtis stood behind the counter asking what can I do for you? Ed said if I find you was behind mu house burning down you will answer to me. Curtis grabbed the gun stuck it in his face then said when I have a package delivered I expect to be paid. Slamming down the envelope Ed gave them.

Now I suggest you shut your mouth and leave Ed thought Curtis was going to be a push over now he was staring down the barrel of a gun. Backing away he left Gwen ask would you have really shot him? Curtis said it is like playing poker. Sometimes you have to bluff them walking over to the customers apologizing for the disturbance.

Nick ask what was that all about? Curtis looked at his wife Nick you can talk in front of her. Curtis told him what happened Nick said if that was me holding the gun he never would have walked out of here. Curtis said now he knows I will not be pushed around Nick smiled Curtis went on to say I think I provide a service that a lot of people can benefit from Nick said you do you have opened up a way where some of us can make more money. a week had past ED was setting down outside watching his wife and daughter play to together they was at a park.

A man named Grey Hauger walked up to ED saying hello Ed said hello sir. Grey introduced himself then he sat down next to Ed he said being a business man myself if I started. Scam my supplier my business would not last long Ed ask did Sandaro send you? Grey said he knows nothing about this.

See with Mr. Sandaro's sharp mind he has opened up a way some of us can get what we want. Mr. Sandaro had and important guest in the store at the some time as your out burst. So your lucky to be setting here with your pretty wife and daughter. The meeting ended and Grey left Ed had no clue Sandaro was supplying some very rough people.

A month later other important guest came in the store it seems their wives were curious. Gwen was there to greet them as they came in Jake and Curtis was finishing up with a shipment. They said good day ma'am they look around the wife said what a charming store. Oh look they have that fruit in a jar I like. She grabbed two jars looking at Gwen she said I love this. Gwen said I like them also but pointing at Curtis and saying he does not.

Her husband saw some whiskey he said Curtis you have whiskey? Curtis said I came across that by accident. The man ask oh how? Curtis said a man was suppose to deliver this to a bar but he did not know the bar burnt down the day before he got there. So he was stuck with load then someone directed him here, I had heard about the bar from other people.

So I bought the load the man ask how is it moving? Curtis not bad the man ask would you add a bottle to our order please. Then they paid Gwen the store was doing better then he thought more and more people were coming in. the items for baking was a hot commodity they made sure to keep them in stock.

It was a couple months later while unloading a truck the driver said while pointing at a crate of can goods. You get that also oh I was told to give you this letter it goes along with it, Curtis said thank you then unloaded the truck and paid the driver the read the letter.

It said dear Mr. Sandaro a person named Ed willowbrock is to be purchasing this crate. The driver will let us know that it was delivered we encourage you to charge this much naming the price as our way of

Black Rose

saying thank you. Now Curtis thought this to be odd then again last time he saw this person he shoved a gun in his face. He told Jake and Gwen about the crate Jake said this is the same guy that cheated us. Curtis held the letter up saying this came along with it he let them read it also. Jake said he got under someones skin Curtis said the people we supply for you do not want to do that.

Ed willowbrock was part of and organized crime family trying to climb the ladder but he slipped up with Curtis, now he was on a thin line. Now he had to make good he had to deliver that crate to a restaurant so he drove out to Sandaro's Trading post walking in Curtis was at the counter. Jake was helping Gwen dust their last face off did not go well Ed ask for the crate. Curtis gave him a stern look then went to get the crate Gwen whispered to Jake both looked at the counter. As Curtis set it down open it up so he could see then sealed it shut Ed handed him and envelope.

Taking it Curtis gave him a dirty look then opened it this time money was in it. Ed said you will find the payment for the crate and the delivery in there Curtis said enjoy the crate thank you for your business. Curtis was always polite to all of his customers but the are times when one crosses the line and rubs you the wrong way.

Ed turned and took the crate to the restaurant it was intended for, by the time he got there the place was about to close. Walking in he ask for the owner Tony Starger Tony came walking out ask how can I help you? Ed said I have something from Sandaro's Trading. Tony said bring it in and set it on this table after setting it on the table Ed said he opened it. Tony said that is what I was looking for he opened it to show you what is inside, he has to know what he is dealing with.

Which is good see one time a competitor found out about my shipment, they went a bought it from Sandaro's Trading he thought he was bringing it here. The next day we came to pick it up Mr. Sandaro said you driver pick it up yesterday. Our men told him sir we are the drivers they saw they caught him off guard. Mr. Sandaro ask who was the man yesterday? My men ask if he could describe him not only did he he also told us what kind of car he drove.

Between what he told us and some rumors we found him then eliminated him. So for no further mistakes he gets a letter with each shipment after the story Tony paid Ed the delivering the crate. It has been two years sense Curtis opened the store and it has been doing very good. In so much he decided to expand it by thirty feet on one side Curtis got the permit. To do it then finding out Cinder his wife was pregnant, by the time the expansion was made Gwen returned from having her baby their mother baby sat. the expansion was filled with the stuff that moved fast and the new items that was slow sellers was put in the old spot. The truck drivers in that area would sometimes have damaged bow or crates. The company they delivered for would not take them boxes so the driver would get stuck with them. If it was food they would take it home anything else they would take to Sandaro's trading to see if they was interested in it. This is where they would come to get rid of their damaged goods and make some money on the side.

Then later that afternoon a police car pulled up out front Curtis ask Gwen is everything out? Gwen said yes the last item was picked up and hour ago. Jake took a couple of them on a delivery Curtis said good the police just pulled up. The two officers walked in one said we heard you have been doing some smuggling. Curtis said really feel free to look around oh how good of a shot are you two officers. See we have a fly that is driving us nuts the two officers looked at each other. one ask would you like us to arrest it almost laughing Curtis walked them through the back of the store. Letting them look in what ever they wanted the two officers left finding nothing saying thank you for your time sir.

CHAPTER 2

Months flew by and Cinder gave birth to a boy they named him Richard Allen Sandaro. Curtis's mother was named Ida she said bring him over here I will watch him. Curtis ask don't you have one to watch after already Ida said so I will have two babies to look after.

There was a truck driver that just got in town he had two stops a grocery store and a warehouse belonging to Scott Zebulon. James Ronald the truck driver stopped for a bit to eat when he finish he used the bathroom. At that time a person jumped in his truck and took off James came out finding his gone. He then called the police to report his truck stolen the police came and took a report. When that was done James called the store and warehouse that he was suppose to deliver to telling them what just happened.

The warehouse called Scott Zebulon who owned it he ran a black market and he had merchandise on the truck. Designated for his warehouse then to the black market this was one way how he made his money. Scott called his men saying get on the streets and find out who just stole my goods filling them in on what happened. Three days went by they found out who took his truck a Tony Wilkens they in turn took Tony in to Scott. Scott said I understand you stole a truck full of stuff! Tony said yes what about it.

Scott said I had a delivery on that truck now the truck driver is out of a job, so you better give me a reason why I should not kill you. Tony said I was paid to steal it Scott said by who? Tony saw things was not going to good for him. A Patrick O' Leary paid me $600 one of Scott's men said hey boss that is one of Brain Metzlor's men. Another one of his men said yeah he runs a chop shop for Metzlor Scott called Brain. Brain said hello how are things? Scott said one of your boys stolen some of my merchandise. Brain said I never ordered it Scott said I have a person who gave me a name.

A Patrick O' Leary Brain said he is one of mine men but I know nothing of the heist. But I will get to the bottom of it and any truth to it he will not do it again. Scott said you have 48 hours before I come in looking for him myself and my stuff. Brain said after hanging up said find that idiot Patrick O'Leary he is about to start another war with Zebulon again one I did not wish to relive.

One of his men said you almost lost the chop shop in that Brain said we have 48 hours. Scott Zebulon called in and anonymous tip to the police where to find the truck. Dusting it for finger prints they found Tony's And Patrick's on it, they arrested Tony for grand theft. They knew Patrick work for Metzlor it was a matter of time before they caught him.

Brain had two honest business's a car lot and a furniture store, then he had his chop shop. Then police came talking to a couple of Metzlor's men they said they saw him a couple of weeks ago trying to through them off. Then in turn they told Brain about the police Brain said dam find Patrick and make him and example. We do not need the police snooping around about that truck twenty hours later Metzlor's men found Patrick, hiding in the chop shop.

Brain and with five of his men swarmed in his men dragging him to a clearing in the shop. Brain hit him hard sending down to the floor he said you little puke because of you I have Scott Zebulon breathing down my neck and the police knocking at my door. Now where is the merchandise you stole? Patrick did not say a word one of his men step on his hand. Saying the boss asked you a question Patrick yelled saying in the back under a trap I was lining up a buyer. Brain told two of his men to go look for it and found it untouched and used this trap to make sure no blood gets on the floor.

Then dump his body somewhere else that way the police will get off my ass, then in the morning get some men load this stuff up and take it to Scott Zebulon this will quiet him down. That night they dumped his body then loaded up the stuff taking it it Zebulon's house. Telling his men they had a delivery for Mr. Zebulon they went and got him Scott said good evening gentlemen how can I help you? One of the men said we found your stolen stuff and we are here to bring it to you. As far as O'Leary well he will not try it again Zebulon said you can put it over there.

When they was finish unloading the men said sir we would like to make a suggestion, we knew this stuff was coming in and if we knew so did the police. We suggest Sandaro's Trading it is a discreet way of getting your stuff how ever it will cost you a little bit. Zebulon thanked the men for his stuff then they left Scott ask his men if anyone of them knew about this place one of his men said yes then explained how it worked. Three days later Scott and his wife went to visit the store they walked in Curtis and Jake was busy trying to catch a mouse.

Gwen greeted then with a hello they looked around when Scott saw a man come in. walking up to the counter where Gwen was at then ask for something but he did not hear what. A package was brought out for him the man pulled out and envelope then laid it on the counter taking the package then left. then heard Jake say got him trapping the mouse in a box both stood up and saw the customers Curtis said we finally caught this mouse after nearly two weeks. As Scott and his wife Eleanor was looking around when she spotted something her grocery did not have that she needed for baking.

She brought it to her husband showing him Scott said our store rarely has that, then looking at Curtis asking him how often do you get this? Curtis said we have truck drivers bring us in broken boxes and crates. Because the people they drive for will not take them this

Black Rose

was one of the products . Scott ask so you will not be getting any more? Curtis said I got this broken case two days ago I had no idea it would sell this fast. Scott said where we shop at they rarely have this Curtis said I ask my delivery man about this yesterday he is suppose to get back with me.

Scott said I am a business man myself recently someone stolen my merchandise. Curtis ask would that have anything to do with a truck? Scott said yes Curtis said sir if you don't mind can we go in back a work out a better way for you Scott said sure. Curtis looked at his wife saying excuse us ma'am if you need anything just ask we will do what we can.

In back Curtis explained how things worked Scott was interested. Scott ask what if I can find that baking goods? Curtis said you would mix your stuff in with that with a note who is picking it up. One of our men can come and get it or we can deliver Scott said Deliver. How do you get paid? Curtis said they give my driver and envelope Scott ask has anyone tried to rip you off? Curtis said yes his house burnt down that same night. Scott smile then said I like your style Mr. Sandaro Curtis said well sir I am trying to provide a special service. Now there has been a few time I would get a shipment and find just a note an d nothing else. No merchandise then I have to call the name in the letter telling them what happened and it is almost always a mess up at the warehouse.

Scott said lets see if we get find this baking stuff and we can start doing business. Curtis said Mr. Zebulon I have heard about your stuff for a while Scott said that was suppose to be a secret. Curtis said according to what I have heard the law was following that truck. They did nor count on someone stealing it Scott said maybe it was a good thing that it was stolen.

They came out shaking hands in turn Scott found out the law was closing in on him. Scott found his wife having a good time talking ti Gwen and Jake, in time Curtis located a company to supply him with the baking stuff. He in turned Called Scott Zebulon telling him Scott invited Curtis and his wife to dinner. So both could talk some business and work thing out the evening went good and plans were set.

Curtis had bought three acres up in the mountains right beside a lake then had a three bedroom cabin built on the land. His youngest brother open up a riding stable which was right down the mountain from the cabin. All the family by know was involved in the smuggling which helped finance the younger brothers riding stable.

Curtis used and amphibious plane to get to the cabin he then had a a dock built. This is where he would take vacations along with the rest of the family members or Curtis would park his car at the riding stables and take a horse up. Which was a five miles ride Curtis also had a secret room built in the cabin.

This is where he kept the guns at to get in you had to move a horse shoe that was hanging on the wall. The family did plenty hunting and fishing then Curtis gathered stones and built a stone grill. The family thought is looked strange but once they began using it then they like it but Curtis all bones from the fish or game cooked was to be buried. Curtis also learned how to tan hides so all the rabbit, deer and bear hides was stole in the stone. But Cinder and Gwen came up with and idea to make hat out of these hides.

They talked to Curtis it sounded interesting to him so the women made a couple from the up coming winter. It was then they found out the hats was good sellers, then one evening Cinder mention to Curtis about wanting a garden. He said we do have some land up by the cabin Cinder said I was talking to some people at work they said the deer are good for ruining gardens. Curtis said hmm that would leave the cabin out but we do have enough here for one Cinder said yes, we do have two acres here. Curtis smiled then said any deer gets in our garden here I am going to shot it they try to eat our garden we eat them.

One day a man walks in and got talking to Jake about Scott Zebulon's deliveries from this store. Curtis and Gwen were busy with customers Charles was unloading a truck. He walks up to Jake he said excuse me Jake ask how can I help you? The man said my name is Larry Barnswell I work for Scott Zebulon. Curtis saw him talk to Jake but something seemed wrong to him Jake said well his wife did call in a list saying they would stop by to pick it up. Other people was coming in Larry said I will stop by later when you are not so busy.

When the people cleared Jake told Curtis about the man telling him he was asking about Mr. Zebulon's shipments. Curtis said I can not explain it but something doesn't feel right, what did you tell him? Jake said that Mr. Zebulon's wife called in a grocery list for her sick mother. Both Gwen and Charles agree this was odd someone asking about them Curtis said wait until Mr. Zebulon comes to get his groceries. A short time later Scott Zebulon walks in to pick up the stuff Curtis gave him a look then ask can we talk? Scott gave him and odd look the followed him in back. Curtis ask do you know a Larry Barnswell? Scott said yes he works for me Curtis said well he was in here this morning asking about your shipments from here.

Scott said I see thank you I will check in to it and solve his problem, right now my mother in law is sick and I need to get these to her. As they walked up front Curtis said I hope she starts to feel better, Scott and his wife spent a couple days there at her mother's house then went back home. When they get home Scott called a couple of his men they meet in private. Scott said I want you guys to find out about this Larry Barnswell one of his men said he works at your clothing store.

Another guy there said yeah that's right he has been there two years, Scott said he has been asking questions I want to know why and who he really is. Two weeks went by before they got back with Scott, Scott ask what did you find out? One of his men said he is a federal agent. Scott said lets show him he has been found out the men went and found his car then cut the brake line.

Getting off from work at the clothing store where he was working under cover, he got in his car. Then left Larry went to stop at and intersection he hit the brakes nothing he was hit by another car hard. The ambulance was called Larry was unconscious in the hospital when his boss showed up. Others agents was there there boss ask anyone knows his condition? Another agent said he is in stable condition. The boss said he is here because his cover was blown another agent said his brake was cut. He said he thought he found out something on

Scott Zebulon their boss said look where it got him. I want his room guarded he is not going back now they know who he is.

A wealthy business man came in town he owned some house's which he rented out and a couple business. He went in a store to buy a couple suits while inside a small time car thief jumped in his car and took off. A couple of police officers show him a went after them the car theft hit the gas, the police radioed in the make and model of the car. He was able to lose the police then he took it to Metzlor's chop shop where he was looking to get a nice price for it. While another police car was going by and noticed the car he found out it was called in stolen. Keeping their sirens off they surround the chop shop shutting down the operation.

A short time later Brain Metzlor was told about the raid, so Brain and some of his men drove by. The police had it sealed off the gates was locked they knew the police would go through everything every inch of the shop. They charged everyone that worked there Brain ask his men see if you can find out what happened to my shop. Brain found out a car theft was trying to make a score and got sloppy he end up getting arrested as well.

One of the men said boss we can open up another shop some place else. Brain said we need to let things calm down first besides they are after me, they was trying for Scott Zebulon. I betting he is the one the put that agent in the hospital one of the men said the news said it was and accident Brain said accident my foot. Here is what I think happened he ask the wrong question to the wrong person. That person told Zebulon that accident was staged to say I found you out. The law knew Brain Metzlor owned the building but could not prove he was in on what was going on inside.

A holiday was coming up all stores would be closed Curtis and family headed to the cabin. Eight people ended up at the cabin the evening before the holiday, the next morning most of them went fishing until two in the afternoon. The rule was all the fish bone was to be buried to keep the bears away. the evening the plane returned to start taking people back Curtis his wife and son were the last. They

Black Rose

was wanting to make sure everything was out and put away before they left.

It was a few days after the holiday when a man came into rob the store, but he did not count on two off duty policemen to be in the store shopping at the time. So there ended up being a stand off for and hour before the robber gave up they hand cuffed the man. then used there phone to call in for a car to come and get this guy after he was taken away Gwen and Jake thank the two police officers. When they got home their wives ask why they was late then they explain to there wives what happened, they wives said I bet they was glad you was there.

It was two weeks later when the TV news said a man escaped from the maximum security prison. They said his name and showed his picture Victor dross if you see him call the police. He is serving life for murder when he was a short distance from the prison he scattered pepper all over his trail. Victor ran until he could not go no more while he was resting he saw some clothing hanging on a line. Noticing some was men's clothes he smiled thinking time to get rid of these. Measuring the pants against him self they look like they would fit he also took a shirt. Throwing his prison cloth in some bushes then taking off three miles down the road he saw a man getting in his car. It was one of Scott Zebulon's men he ask him for a ride it which he got turned down. Victor attack him he noticed a gun he grabbed it then shot him the other began to run Victor shook his head.

Then got and the car and taking off the other man ran inside and called the police. When the police got there they took a report not only from him but from other witness as well. The police ask can you describe the man. Scott's man said it is the guy you showed on TV going to his car the officer grabbed a wanted poster and showed him. Afterwards the man called Scott in turn he sent someone down to pick him up, Then paid for the funeral for one of his men.

Victor robber a store to get some money to eat on after he ate he found a place to park the car for the evening. In the morning Victor drove until he ran out of gas figuring the police would be looking for it he left on foot. Now there was a building be built across the road from Sandaro's Trading and it was just about done, the construction crew had left for the evening.

Victor was just about near Sandaro's Trading when he saw the patrol car pass him. Turning his head in hopes he would not be recognized the patrol car slowed down after passing him. One officer said that was Victor Dross they went to turn around after passing him. Victor ran inside the empty building they saw where he went then called for back up. Curtis, Gwen and Jake heard several police sirens looking out the window they was surrounding the building across the street. Charles just got back from a delivery asking the police what was going on? They told him to stay back saying nothing more.

Charles went in the store asking them what is going on over there? Jake said they have Victor Dross held up in the building. Looking in back of the building Victor saw he was boxed in so he went to the front of the building. Victor shot two officers before being shot himself the second bullet killed him. They waited several minutes before going in the ones in back of the building went in first. The found Victor dead with two bullets in him they yelled out we found him he is dead, Then they radioed for a corner to come and get the body.

Curtis said wait they come in the morning Jake said they are going to cry they closed the store for the night. They wanted to be open to see the face on the construction's face, the crew finally got there to see bullet holes all over the place and blood on the floor. A couple of them went to Sandaro's Trading to see if they knew what happened. Curtis said the police had a shoot out with Victor Dross yesterday evening, the crew then ask if they could use the phone. So they called the owner of the building telling him what happened a short time later the owner showed up to see the bullet holes.

The owner went across the street to ask Sandaro's Trading what they knew then headed to the police station. Demanding to speak to how was in charge from there he went to the mayor of the city. And had a lengthy conversation on the repairs to his building when Scott saw Victor was dead he called off his men. The police got to him before Scott Zebulon did he wanted him dead for killing one of his men and stealing one of his cars.

Cinder got pregnant a second time she Quit her job to be a full time mother. Richard was two years old when his brother was born he was five when his sister Emma was born. Curtis and Cinder stopped at three. Now that building across the street from Sandaro's Trading was now a restaurant with a guest that did not want to leave. A truck driver pull to the farthest part of Sandaro's Trading parking lot then went inside to see if it was OK to park his truck there while he went across the street to eat.They gave him permission he said thank you then left, after he ate he was crossing the street and got hit by a car.

When the ambulance got thee to check him out the loaded him up he died on the way to the hospital. Curtis told the police the truck belong to the man hit by the car so and officer and Curtis went looking through the cab for any kind of paper work. Saying where he was going they finally found it Brain Metzlor Curtis said I know this guy. The officer said if you know him how about telling him about his delivery.

Curtis ask can he take the truck the officer said yes we know where to find him, Curtis called Brain after the police left. Brain said hello Curtis said this is Curtis Sandaro Brain said hello how are things going? Curtis ask are you expecting a delivery ? Brain said yes sometime today. Curtis said well your driver just got hit by a car his truck is parked in my parking lot. Brain ask what police department? Curtis told him Brain in turn called the police asking about the driver. And was told he died on the way to the hospital Brain ask if he could send a driver to get his truck. They gave him the go ahead it took a full day to find a another driver to get that truck to bring his supplies to him.

CHAPTER 3

Charles came back from the delivery telling Curtis how a knew customer stuck a gun in his face. The man's name was Tucker Flanner he was a big on extortion and demanding protection money, from business or he would destroy them. Curtis called tucker asking him about this? Tucker said that is how I keep them honest. Curtis said sir the amount of time I have been doing this I found out the person holding the gun is not honest. Tucker said I tell you what give me this amount of money and nothing happens to your store. Curtis told him to shove it then hung up on him Gwen ask what is going on? Curtis said he is demanding protection money.

Jake ask what are you going to do? Curtis said fight fire with fire. one thing about Curtis when he starts doing business with you he find out all you illegal activities. So Curtis grabbed and empty pop bottle filled it fill of gas then stuck a piece of clothes in the top. It was ready for tonight then he ask for tuckers address Charlie handed it to him. Curtis smiled saying thank you that night after his wife and children went to bed. He told Cinder he had to take off of some business so he put on some boots that were to big for him. There boot he wore to clean out the barns with.

Curtis left at 12:30 am after a nice drive he found the place he had park in a dark spot, then walked around Tucker land. Spotting a building out back Curtis smiled walking up to it at throwing range. Lighting the wick he threw it catching the building in fire then he ran and took off turning his lights on when he was a good distance away. Tucker woke up to see his build engulfed in flames, by the time the fire department got there and put out the flames the building was a total lose. In the morning they came back looked around and said it was arson they could not find not tracks.

A few days later Tucker called Curtis with the same demand, Curtis hung up on him. Then calling the police to report some back room gambling by Tucker Flanner. The officer said to the other hey guys just got a tip on Tucker Flanner another officer said we would love to bust him, but everyone is afraid to talk. The officer the answered the phone held a piece of paper up saying here is two addresses someone just called in on him.

Everyone left but the dispatcher separating both addresses on the count of three they kicked in the doors, arresting everyone and took all the paper work. Word got out the next morning it was told to Tucker about the two raids he got very upset. First his building now his gambling rooms something clicked Curtis Sandaro, then hearing on the TV about the two raids Scott Zebulon and Brain Metzlor smiled.

Both had heard he was trying to put the squeeze on Curtis and both men knew Curtis to well. The investigators was looking through all the paper work from the two raids. Brain had heard Tucker was going to hit Sandaro's Trading so he called the store to inform them. Curtis staked out the store parking around back where no one could see him. He could not use a gun with the restaurant across the street he might hit one in the parking lot and they would hear.

So he used a sling shot found some rocks then waited three days went by when a car pulled up a little after dark. Right before the restaurant closed for the night a man stepped out of a car then lite a wick to a bottle. Curtis figured to hit him in the face he had become a good shot with it he had been playing with it sense he was a kid. The man went to throw the bottle Curtis released his sling shot the rock curved and hit the bottle, spilling the gas all over the man catching him on fire.

Curtis erased his tracks and left while a couple of customers at the restaurant called a waitress saying there is a man on fire over there. The manager and along with some waitresses filled some buckets up rushed over dumping it on the fire. They then called the police the man died before the life squad got there, the next morning on the news it said a man caught himself on fire in the Sandaro's Trading parking lot. Tucker was watching the news at the time he said what the hell happened ? The police called Curtis that night telling him what happened. Curtis ask do I need to do anything? The police said no sir you do not we think it was arson gone wrong.

Tucker sat there wondering what happened? How did he catch him self on fire? So he decided to go for lunch. Ended up going to the restaurant across the street from Sandaro's Trading. Jake walked out to get the mail when he saw Tucker Flanner pull in. walking back inside he told Curtis hey guess what besides mail Flanner is eating across the street.

Curtis said he was probably trying to figure how his man caught on fire. Jake ask how do you know it was his man? Curtis said he had a Molotov cocktail . He tried to burn down the store Gwen ask how did he catch on fire? Curtis told them what happened, then waited by the window for Tucker to come out.

When Tucker walked out to go to his car so Curtis stepped out of the store and stopped. both men looked at each other Charlies saw Tucker as he pulled in from a delivery. Getting out of his car asking Curtis what is he doing here? Curtis said he is eating and wondering. Charlies ask then what are you doing? Curtis said showing him I will not put up with his shit. Tucker left a few minutes later a few week passed when Charlies had a delivery to make out that way. He came upon some rope sense he had no more deliveries and it was near the time when the store was to close.

Black Rose

He stopped in on a friend of his to visit around eleven at night he went to go leave. He ask his friend if he would play look out for him Jim ask why what is up? Charlie said have you heard of Tucker Flanner? Jim said who has not heard of that gangster! Charlie said he is trying to take over the store. I got thinking about putting this rope around his driveshaft so they left Charlie crawled under the car tying it off on the front axle then they left.

In the morning Tucker his wife and his two sons was going somewhere, when has he heard a noise under the car then it stopped. he got out to take a looked finding his drive shaft laying on the ground. Eventually he got some help and his wife and kids was taken back home. Tucker called Curtis saying Mr. Sandaro if I find you sabotage my car your dead. Curtis said Mr. Flanner what are you talking about? Tucker said someone sabotage my car causing the drive shaft to fall off. I am wanting to think it was you Curtis said your fishing with your line of work you have made lots of enemies. Then Curtis hung up on him Charlie was giving direction to someone that was lost. When they left Charlie ask who was burning your ear up? Curtis said Tucker he is trying to finger me for sabotaging his car.

Charlie smiled and never said a word mean while Tucker was getting some guns ready. He was gearing up for a drive by, but the day before it was suppose to take place. The police came knocking on his door and arrested him for tax evasion that evening the news announced gangster Tucker Flanner was arrested on tax evasion.

Both Scott and Brain was shocked and cheering at that same time, Brain called Curtis asking would you know who took Tucker Flanner down almost laughing. All Curtis said this is my store and no one is going to take it from me, once Tucker was arrested many people came forward telling the police they was forced to give him protection money.

Months went by when a warehouse was doing inventory they discovered a large inventory of boxes of make up. Then looking through the records to find out they have been setting there for eight months. While management was trying to figure out what happened a drive pulled in to get a load. While loading his truck a employee was telling him about the boxes of make up. The truck driver said try calling Sandaro's Trading they by odd stuff sometimes even for us truckers.

I deliver to the store he might buy it all from you, after he was loaded and drove away the employee told his boss what the driver said. When management heard this they called Sandaro's Trading Gwen called Curtis to the phone. Their offer did sound good Curtis said I would like to see this before a say anything. After hanging up he told Gwen and Jake that after he opens in the morning he is going to see this offer. Then told them what it was Gwen teased him by saying I an running out. The next day around eleven Curtis got to this company a supervisor welcomed him Curtis ask for a list of what it was.

Then the supervisor took him to go see the stuff, Curtis was surprised on how much there was. As big as the building was he understood how it could have got lost. Curtis took there offer and told them he would send a truck to come and get it. When he got back to the store he showed then the list Jake was shocked asking where are we going to put all this at.

Curtis said this is why I am going to call Scott Zebulon to see if he would like to buy some off of me, he is in the black market. A couple of days later a truck pulled in to unload and he had a nice size truck. While helping him unload Curtis hired him to go pick up the stuff he just bought. The truck drive said well Mr. Sandaro I do not have anything after this Curtis ask him can you get for me tomorrow? The drive said I will get it first thing in the morning. Over the years Curtis had improved on the store one of them was adding loading docks, this is where the truck driver would back there trucks u to to unload.

This was right before lunch Jake suggested to the driver that he should get some lunch. They was about to eat theirs so he walked across the street then after lunch with there bellies full they unloaded the truck by hand. Which end up taking sometime then he paid the driver saying thank you. When Curtis rested up he separated what he would need to double his profit. Right before the store closed Gwen went through the shipment of make up and resupplied her. Curtis was tired when he got home cinder filled him in on how Richard was doing in school.

Opening up the next day the three of them looked over the store for a place to set the make up. When they finally settled on a spot Gwen and Jake began filling the space while Curtis called Scott Zebulon to offer him some of the shipment. Scott had a couple of business's that he made money on but they was also fronts he also ran a black market. So a couple of his men along with him drove over to the store to see what Curtis had to offer.

Scott and his men walked in the store greeting Curtis,Gwen and Jake like old friends. Curtis wave he was on the phone Gwen said hello Mr. Zebulon can I help you? Scott said Curtis called me on some Boxes of make up. Gwen said we have some on the shelf right over here walking him over to where they were at. Gwen said I updated my make up I was running low Scott smiled saying my wife might do the same thing.

When Curtis got off the phone he looked at Jake saying I thought she was going to talk my ear off. One of Scott's men said your mother Curtis said no my aunt I have no idea where she gets so much to talk about. One of his men said for me it is my mother Curtis ask where did Scott go? One of his men said in back with Gwen Curtis went to go join them.

Curtis went back and joined them hearing Gwen talk about the stuff he was hoping to sell them. Gwen and Scott saw Curtis coming he ask Scott what do you think? Scott said with seeing how it looks like on Gwen and she has a good sales pitch. I will take half of your extra stock if it moves then I will come back for the rest Curtis said thank you I have enough to double my profit.

Besides this will free up needed storage space Scott ask have you thought about expanding? Curtis I thought about it and that as far as it went, when I got the phone call asking me if I would be interested I did not think it would be this much. Things smoothed over and his business picked and his children grew, soon he was watching his eldest son graduate thinking where did time go he grew so fast.

Joe now sixteen ask his dad if he could learn to fly a plane? Curtis ask why would you want to become a pilot? Joe ask dad aren't you curious what it looks like up there? With a little smile Curtis said no. Joe said please dad Curtis said I will think on it, so while at the store Curtis got talking to Gwen, Jake and Charlie about Joe wanting to be a pilot.

Charlie said not a bad idea it could help in business Curtis said what if the plane crashes? Jake said we could move some things around a little faster Rather then use trucks. Gwen said maybe by using a plane to transport some of our stuff in might help ease up on the slower selling items that are on the shelf. Curtis said you all have good ideas with time changing we are going to have to adopt. Looks like this family is going to have it's first pilot just then Richard walked in the store. Gwen said hi Ricky what are you up to? Richard said about six foot. Gwen said one of these days I am going to smack you and that smart mouth.

Richard said dad I have and idea Curtis ask will it cost me money? Richard said if you like it. Curtis trying to hide his smile said I don't like it already Richard said you have not even heard it. Jake said lets hear it Richard said you know that two story building that is empty telling them the location. Jake said that used to be a furniture store Richard said what if it was a restaurant? The four of them looks at each other.

Curtis ask Gwen is that the building right down the road from you? Gwen said I think so describe it Richard. So he did Gwen said yes that is the one Charlie said I want to hear him out this should be interesting. Richard said I have told my idea to a few clients Curtis ask why did not you come to me first? Richard said dad if your clients did not like it there would no sense of telling you. Jake said he has a point! Curtis said go on lets hear it Richard said I was thinking of a BBQ type restaurant, the sloppy kind. The first floor is where the people would come in and eat, the second floor can be for reservation like groups and for our clients.

This way we can talk business to them away from the phone and people. Charlie ask what would we call it? Richard said the BBQ

Black Rose

pit Curtis said we would have to get some recipes. Richard said be right back going to the car into the glove box and pulling out a dozen recipes then taking them inside and showing them. Curtis ask where did you get these? Richard said from our clients look at this one it is from Louisiana it is spicy. This one is sweet the four of them looked through all the recipes Curtis said they really like this! If it is real messy they will ruin there clothes. Richard said not if the waitress tie a bib on them Gwen said that would make them feel special.

Curtis said OK lets go look at this building, before Curtis left he said hold down the fort. Driving down to look at the building they pulled in the parking lot got out and began looking it over. Curtis said this closed two years ago Richard ask why? Curtis said the man that started it died after twenty five years in business, his kids wanted nothing to do with it.

Then looked in the windows the inside looked in good shape, then looking over the parking lot Curtis like what he saw. Then told Richard he would check into it with a little searching Curtis found the family that owned it. Curtis told them he was interested in the building and wanted to buy it, the family decide to sell it because they wanted nothing more to do with it.

The next day Curtis bought the building once the keys were in his hands he said to Richard come on lets go look at it. Holding the keys up they both went back to the building this time going inside. While looking around they noticed stairs going to the second floor Curtis was watching Richard gathering his thoughts, what was he going to come up with.

Richard was standing on the right side then said dad why don't we have the kitchen over here. Curtis ask why? Richard said this side is smaller the kitchen will take up most of the room along with counter space. The other side can be for booths and tables Curtis smiled liking the idea. Richard barley missed being the valedictorian so he knew Richard had a sharp mind. Curtis said the show case window can go for more floor space then they went upstairs, to see how it looked which was not in bad shape.

Noticing a few leaks in the ceiling Curtis was wondering how old the roof was. Two hours had passed when they headed back to the store Gwen ask well how did it look? Curtis said not bad for and old building. It needs a roof and got some ideas now I need two things a roofer and and architect. Gwen pulled out the phone book and said here start looking after some time looking he found the numbers he needed.

During dinner that evening he gave his approval for flying lessons he said there s a catch. Joe ask what is that dad? Curtis said if we need to move something you will used the plane. When dinner was done Curtis and the boys went to watch TV while Emma and her mother washed the dishes. Curtis wanted more coffee walking in the kitchen Emma did not notice he walked up behind her. He grabbed her sides Emma let out a scream she said daddy you scared the tar out of me Curtis just laughed.

CHAPTER 4

The next morning from the store Curtis called a roofer and architect. He made both appointments the same day and hour apart, the boss from the roofing company got there first. Curtis took him to the second floor showing him the leaks Tim was the boss for the roofing company he said might be small here but big on top. Curtis said I do not think this roof has ever been replaced Tim ask do you know how old the building is? Curtis said it was built in 1875. Tim said if this is the original roof it is long over due I would like to see what it looks like on top Curtis help yourself.

Tim took his ladder off his truck then climbed to the roof while another car pulled in the parking lot. A man got out asking do you know Curtis Sandaro I am Ryan the architect Curtis said that would be me sir. They shook hands Curtis said come on I will show you and tell your our idea for this place. As Ryan and Curtis was going through the building Tim came down calling for Curtis. Tim said Mr. Sandaro Curtis said over here he then introduced Tim and Ryan then ask how did it look? Tim said not good that roof has never been replace. I can take the job but I will need a few days we are presently on a job site. Curtis said no problem here is my number to get a hold of me then Tim said see you later sir then left.

Ryan and Curtis spent three hours going over the look of the restaurant. Then Curtis went back to the store and Ryan went to work on the draws for the restaurant Richard and Charlie was unloading a truck. It was three days later Tim Martin and his crew got to the knew job site Tim told his crew. This has never been replaced so watch your step up there we are going to have to strip it down. They got to work and after several days they finished the roof he then went and told Curtis in turn he was paid.

It was around three months later Ryan walked in the store with the plans ask for Curtis. Gwen called him from in back when Curtis saw him he said hello Mr. Clarkson how are you doing? Ryan said I have the plans ready for you to see. Curtis said just lay them our over here on the counter everyone gathered around to see this. Has Ryan explained everything as these windows are big I set some tables by them so people can eat and look out.

Jake said so your removing the show case part? Richard said yes dad and I thought people might want to look out the window and eat. Gwen teased Richard you talk like your the boss then smiled Richard said I just ideas is all Curtis said that is why he is going to be the manager. Richard looked at his dad in shock saying dad I have no college degree, Curtis said some of these college kids have no common sense A lot of these business owners have no college.

As Ryan went on to explain everything they liked what they heard, Richard said I have a thought when it rains people come in there shoes will be wet they might fall. Curtis said hmm we have that problem here what if we put a long narrow rug in front of the door.

Curtis said I will call the contractor that worked on the store here to see if he wants this job. Ryan looked around Gwen said this place has been expanded twice Curtis thank Ryan paying him. When he left Richard said dad there will be times I will need your advice Curtis smiled then said I will be right here if ever you need like I always have been, now lets pick out the BBQ sauces.

Curtis called Rowans contractors Philip answer saying hello Curtis said hello this Curtis Sandaro you worked on my store. Philip said oh yes how can I help you? Curtis said I have a big job if you are interested. Philip ask what would that be? Curtis said you know that old furniture store naming the location. Philip said oh yes that place has been close I think three years Curtis said I bought it and I want to turn it into a restaurant.

Philip said your kidding can you wait until we get this job done? Curtis said come to the store when you are ready. It was three weeks later when Philip Rowan came walking in the store Jake said Mr. Rowan how can we help you? Philip said looking for Curtis something about a restaurant. Jake pulled the blue prints from under the counter as Philip was looking then over her went to get Curtis.

Minutes later Curtis and Richard came around the corner Philip saw then and said this is very interesting. Curtis said you do not have to worry about gutting the building except for the window display. Philip said I see Curtis ask how would you like to see what your dealing with? Philip said sure I will give me a better idea what I am getting myself into.

Curtis looked at Richard and said why don't you take him over there Richard said sir if you will follow me. Philip rolled up the blue prints and took them with him as they left Gwen said your taking a big gamble! Curtis said yes just as I did for this place. But the location of the building and the size of the parking lot along being the only one of it's kind.

Charlie ask what was the building at first? Curtis said I do not have a clue I will have to do some digging. Richard and Philip arrived at the building Philip said I forgot about this place. They did a walk through so Philip could get a better perspective with the blue prints which were in his hand. The next day Philip called and ordered all the supplies which would take a couple days. While Curtis went to the county records to look up what his new building was at first. He found the original lay out of the place saying it was built in 1875 when it first opened up as a brothel.

After three days of searching it paid off then looking at the time Curtis went back to the store. Walking in Curtis said you would not believe what it first was Jake said let hear it. Richard just got back from a run he said hey folks any more runs? Gwen said your dad is just about to tell us what his new building was when it first opened.

Curtis looked around everyone was hear then said it was a brothel they all looked at each other. Richard said a brothel! Jake said yes in other word a whorehouse, Richard smiled then said now this will make for some interesting conversation Like was doing what and where. Gwen said eww image eating where people was having sex at Charlie ask Richard what are your plans for tonight? Richard said I have a date with Connie tonight.

Gwen ask how long have you two been dating Richard said a year now. The store closed at five thirty that gave Richard time to go home and shower and change clothes He had to pick Connie up at six thirty. They went out to dinner then after words he took her to what was going to be the restaurant. When the restaurant was half way done Connie and her mother Francine came to the store. Richard had been back ten minutes he saw Connie they talked for a few minutes.

Connie ask is your father hiring for the restaurant yet? Richard said not yet. Connie ask think he would get upset if I ask? Richard said dad no Connie said I will let you get back to work then walked over to Curtis. Saying me Mr. Sandaro Curtis said yes Connie, Connie ask are you doing any hiring for the restaurant ? Curtis thought to tease her. He ask is it the job you want or my son? Connie smiled say both would be fine. Gwen giggled Curtis said I will keep you in mind when I begin to hire, just then Francine called Connie where did you go? Connie said over here mom.

Francine said you are suppose to be helping !Connie said sorry mom I was trying for a job, Francine ask for what? Connie said there restaurant. Francine ask don't you think you should wait until they open? Connie said no time like the present she finished helping her mother and they left. Jake said she is a go getter Curtis said yes she sure is I am wondering if I hired her, if them two would conflict.

Gwen said I have been watching them two I think they would work well together.

Three months later Philip walked in the store smiling saying done. So they closed a little early and everyone headed down to the restaurant .to see what it looked like Charlie said whoa this place is big can I suggest a hostess Curtis said I agree the waitresses will be busy.

Richard sat at one of the tables looking around, Jake ask what are you doing? Richard said trying to see things from a customers viewpoint. Then Gwen sat down and looked around saying I like this and these big window set things off. Curtis said now we can unload the back room of the store Richard got up headed to the storage room it was huge. The rest followed Charlie ask what is this Richard said this is the storage room. Then said dad there is a pig farm around here Curtis said I already talked to him and a large cattle farmer. Jake said that is freaky you two thinking the same way Richard said just think BBQ pork rinds as they went up stairs Curtis said as they looked around let Connie know she is hire Richard.

Gwen ask would you like some help with the hiring? Curtis said I had in mind to hire mostly family. Then looking out the second floor window seeing a sign the read The BBQ pit. So the hiring began and the trucks rolled in Connie was there to help out. Along with the family to help set the place up slowly everything came in to shape.

Richard and his crew went home every evening tired over time everything was ready and the grand opening was set. Two hours before the opening the hours was 10:30 through 10 at night. Curtis and Richard waked through the kitchen to see how things was going. The one cooking the ribs ask Richard are you sure you got this? Richard said if I go crazy I will take you with me.

Richard gather the waitresses and bus boys together for a meeting Curtis was watching to see how he was going to handle things. Richard said we have two hours just to remind everyone When someone orders BBQ you tie the bib around them give one to lay on there lap. Bus boys if thing get busy please help with the bibs and do not forget to look at your schedule. And cover the ones on there breaks lets make sure everything is set before the doors open and goo luck.

They have been advertising for months about the restaurant, there was a sign by the stairs reservation only pointing up stairs. Curtis and Richard had the keys to the front door then the time came it began slow then picked up throughout the day. The customers that ordered the ribs got a surprise when they had bibs tied around there necks and one to place on there laps.

When they saw how messy the ribs was then they understood with a stack of napkins was place on the table. Where there was families the put a bowel of pork rinds for them to snack on while waiting for there order. The person covering the cash register was told no more then fifty dollars in the draw the rest goes in a metal box below with a hole in the top.

Curtis had two managers Richard his son and a niece that went to college for book keeping. Richard would leave at five pm she would replace him Courtney was her name she would come in at four thirty so Richard could fill her in. Connie got off at the same time as Richard he ask where she was wanting to eat? Connie said why not here. Richard said looked at the crowd then said there is no one up stairs, he then place their orders telling the waitress they will be up stairs.

They went up stairs and found themselves a table but did not have to wait long. While eating Connie said it is so nice to get off my feet Richard said I hear you how was the tipping? Connie said they were tipping good. When they was finished and cleaned off the BBQ Richard got the bill left a nice tip then paid the bill. Her mother and father was there waiting having dinner Francine ask how was your first day of work? Connie said it was crazy and my feet are killing me.

Francine said the food is good Connie ask how do you know? Francine said your father and I had our dinner here. We was wanting to see how the food was he got the Louisiana BBQ was, but he was not ready how spicy it was. Connie laughed saying daddy's mouth must be on fire how much water did he drink? Francine said a lot.

Soon some of Curtis's clients or people he does business with begin calling and reserving tables up stairs, they wanted to see how the food was. Finding out the food was quite good and the bibs was humorous until they got there meal and saw how messy it was going to be. As they ate they understood the stack of napkins and the little wet towels during Joe's third solo flight as a pilot someone ask who was that, that just took off? The second person said that is Joe Sandaro. The first person said why does that name sound familiar? The second person said Curtis Sandaro is his father he has Sandaro's Trading and now a restaurant. A Sam wheeler got word of Joe being a pilot and found out how to get in touch with the family Driving to the BBQ pit Richard was just finishing his lunch when his dad just called saying he was on his way over for lunch, Also to get a take out for Gwen, Jake and Charlie. Sam told the hostess I want to speak to Rose please the hostess said yes sir follow me please. taking him up stairs then setting him at a table she said I will get you a waitress and a person to talk to.

After leaving the hostess found the waitress then ask for Richard, she said he is in the kitchen. He was giving his dishes to the dish washer. She then told him about the man up stairs Richard ask show me where he is. He also my father will be here anytime she then pointed the guest out, Richard walked up to the man as the waitress gave him the menu and a glass of water. Richard said I am Richard Sandaro how can I help you? Sam said I need a pilot. Richard I have a brother that is a pilot just then Curtis walked in the hostess said up stairs go right.

Curtis said I would like a pull pork sandwich with spicy BBQ and a order of fries, here is a list for three take out meals nothing like business during lunch. The waitress was heading upstairs to see if the guest was ready to order and took Curtis with her. The waitress ask are you ready to order sir? Sam said I will have to BBQ chicken dinner with the sweet BBQ. When she left Richard said this is my father then he introduced both men, he fill his father in on what Sam was looking for. Turning to Sam if you will excuse me sir I need to get back my father will take it from here.

Curtis ask mind if I join you? Sam said go right a head setting down Curtis said so you need a pilot. Sam said yes as he saw the waitress come back with his food after she put it down she said you will need this so she tied it around his neck then said if you will sir

Black Rose

place this one on your lap. Then giving Curtis his food Curtis ask what is with the small bowl of ketchup and BBQ sauce? The waitress said remember when that truck was late well Richard was thinking fast put some BBQ in a bowl took it to the customers explaining about the later truck. Now the request for BBQ sauce is as much as ketchup for there fries enjoy your meals gentlemen.

Laying down a stack of napkins then left Sam said your son has a good head on his shoulders. They talked business while eating then a man came in asking to speak to the manager. The hostess said I can take you to his office the man said I wish to order as well. The hostess took him to a table at the top of the stairs then went to go get Richard. Sam said to Curtis that man over there is a police officer Curtis ask who? Sam pointed him out.

Richard came up stairs saying hello officer how are you doing? The man was surprised saying you must be mistaken. Richard said no I was working for Sandaro's Trading before landing this job. I made deliveries to busy people and the elderly I saw you one day in Elkton making and arrest. Curtis' back was toward the officer so he did not see him the officer said that is why I am here I heard he is in to smuggling. Richard said sir I also unloaded trucks he tried to tell me it build character but that is not what my back said when I got done. The officer left while Curtis was laughing Richard walked over asking how was the food Sam said the food is delicious.

Richard said I will tell the cook Sam said the bib are a great idea and he is leaving Richard said that was rude he did not even order. Oh by the way two apple pies was just taken out of the oven a scoop of ice cream will set it off. Sam said that does sound good Richard ask would you like me to send your waitress back up? Sam said yes it will give me time to clean up. Sam gave Curtis the coordinates Curtis looked at a bunch of numbers that did not make sense. The waitress came back up to add a slice of apple pie to his order Curtis joined him.

After they was done Sam got his bill then left first Curtis picked up his orders then left for the store. That evening at home he told Joe you have your first run handing him the paper with the numbers on it and a name. Joe said this is a pick up Curtis said yes and that contact starts at the time when shown on the paper. Joe teased his dad saying want to come along dad I can show you how to do a barrel roll. Curtis said no I an keeping my feet on the ground Emma his youngest said daddy it is fun. He took me up a couple times Curtis smiled saying no my feet stays on the ground.

That Saturday Joe goes to the airport and gets a plane while doing a check up a man comes up. Saying doing a check list Joe said yes I want to make sure everything is alright before I go up. The man said my name is Ed that stuck Joe the name on the paper Joe ask your you my contact here? Ed said my father gave you some numbers. Joe said yes I have them right here ED said them numbers are to a home made airport. Joe gave him a look ED laugh saying don't worry it is safe crop dusters use it. The check list came up good Joe was in the sir in no time punching in the numbers given him.

After some time in the air he saw his destination the run way looked good from the air. Circling the area before he landed then asking for Wendell, they shook hands Wendell then showing Joe a box picking it up Wendell walked it over placing it in the plane. This was Joe's first time taking off from a home made run way it was a little rough but he was able to take off. Wendell had called Ed telling him Joe is on his way a short time later he was landing. Joe smiled when he saw Ed waiting as soon as the plane stopped Ed went to greet him . Unloading the merchandise then handing Joe and envelope with money in it Joe thank him then took it to his father.

Curtis ask how did it go? Joe said it went good the run way was a little rough. Jake ask why was that? Joe said it is a home made one for crop dusters. Curtis took three hundred out and gave it to Joe after that things began to pick up for Joe but his father paid him well.

Richard always made sure Connie his girlfriend got off the same time as him. It was a Saturday Connie had some things to do wither parents Richard had made some reservation for a table on the second floor. For his and Connie's dinner tonight Richard sat around the house most of that day. Cinder ask him are you just going to set around all day Richard mom it feels so good to set and doing nothing. Cinder smiled then said you do not know how close your father came turning down your idea. Richard ask you mean the restaurant mom? Cinder said yes until he got thinking of your big idea. That is why he went through with it Richard said I never thought it was going to take off like this.

Connie's parents names were Mike and Audrey her father ask any plans for tonight? Connie said yes dinner and a movie with Richard. Mike said speaking of him when you two getting married? Connie said daddy sound like you are trying to get rid of me! Audrey said it is not that you two have been dating for two years now.

Connie said I have been so busy with work it went by fast, they got done visiting her grandparents. Then when they got home she called Richard telling him she would be ready. Arriving at her house a few minutes early then knocking on the door Audrey let him in. Connie said to Richard let me use the bathroom before we go Richard smiled saying OK. Looking at Mike he said sir I want your permission for Connie's hand in marriage. Mike said I never thought you was going to ask Richard smile showed him the ring before she came out, Audrey ask when are you gong to ask her? Richard said dinner tonight.

Mike said you have it Connie came out say I am ready then they left driving to the BBQ. Where he made their reservations Connie looked at Richard as they was being taken up stairs she was not expecting this. They was given a table away from the party that would be up in and hour and a half. Then the waitress came up both knew what they wanted so she took the order. Looking around no one he pulled a small box out moved his chair got down on one knee, then said I know we have been busy but I want you for the rest of my life will you marry me? showing her the ring. Connie was shocked with tears she said yes when the waitress came back with their food she saw the ring asking when did you get that? Connie said just now?

The waitress looked at Richard saying you finally did it she left and told the others. They all knew both of them Connie got the chicken dinner Richard ordered the ribs. They took there time eating cleaning up was a different matter, after there dessert they left as Richard was paying for it they had to see her engagement ring.

CHAPTER 5

Fourteen months later the church doors were open and Richard was standing at the alter. The music began Connie and her father approached the aisle and with a hand signal they began the walk. The wedding went off without a hitch Richard had bought a two bedroom house a couple months before the wedding.

The was six acres along with the house the land was cheap back then. eleven months later Connie got pregnant a few months into the pregnancy while being checked out by the doctor. He said I think I hear three heart beats we will have to wait until your farther along. Connie looked at him in shock twins! Then going out to her husband looking in disbelief. Richard ask what is wrong? Connie ask are there twins in your family? Richard said I do not know we can stop by the store and ask my dad.

We pass it up on the way home so they pulled in the parking lot then went in, after a customer left Richard ask Gwen. Aunt Gwen where is dad? Gwen said in back doing inventory Connie placing her hands on her belly. Richard ask do you know if there are twins in the

Black Rose

family Gwen said no not that I know of. Connie said the doctor thinks he heard three heart beats I might be having twins.

Gwen, Jake and Charlie all looked at her after a few minutes of silence, Charlie said oh wait until I tell Curtis. He goes in back looking for him Charlie said hey Richard and Connie are up front. Curtis said OK just about done here Charlie said almost laughing there might be twins in the family. Curtis said no there is not Charlie said Connie might be carrying them. Curtis looked at him Charlie smiled saying yes you heard me right. Curtis stopped what he was doing then went up front Richard said hi dad, Curtis said what is this I hear Connie said said the doctor thinks he heard three heart beats.

A few months passed before the doctor was able to confirm that she was indeed having twins. The news spread fast throughout the restaurant everyone was keeping and eye on her. Soon her belly got big enough to where she could not bend over if she dropped something a bus boy or someone else had to pick it up for her. Around the house Richard would look after her it got the the point he had to put her shoes on her. It was not long before the doctor said she could not work, Cinder her mother in law and her mother took turns watching her and helping her around the house. Setting down was easy it was getting up was the hard part Connie needed help with that.

The day came it was during a shift change Richard was filling in the second shift manager. When the phone rang a waitress picked it up saying the BBQ pit Cinder ask is Richard still there? The waitress said yes aunt Cinder. He is briefing the on coming manager Cinder ask may I speak to him please? The waitress found him saying phone call for you it's your mother. Richard picked it up the phone saying hi mom Cinder said Connie's water just broke I am taking her to the hospital. Richard said I will meet you there then hung up the waitress which was his cousin ask everything OK? Richard said Connie's water just broke. Do me a favor call and tell the store the he rushed to the hospital lucky no police was around as fast as he was going.

Then some hours later Connie gave birth to twins girls their names were Kendall and Kendra Sandaro . A nurse in the delivery room out and ankle bracelet on Kendall sense she was the first and so they could tell who was who the girls was identical.

The nurse's found out fast as long as the twins were in the same crib together they was as good as gold, but when separated for a diaper change they had a fit. They told the parents about when they brought the babies in the room. Most of the family came too visit Connie and the twins while she was in the hospital. Taking all kinds of picture everyone was asking who was who Richard said the one with the ankle bracelet in Kendall the other is Kendra.

Connie was in the hospital a week before being allowed to go home Kendall and Kendra was nice and healthy. Now loading the twins in the car was tricky each parent put one in the car. On the way home Connie said I am going to put nail polish on Kendall's big toe or I will never be able to tell them apart. Richard laughed saying we are going to have fun we need to figure how to tell them apart. Connie said our mothers said they would help while your at work Richard oh good less stress on you.

When they got home Richard pulled in the driveway there was some cars there waiting for them to get home. Nothing like family they helped bring in the diaper bags while Richard and Connie got the twins. Their mother took the twins from them and laid them one in each crib ten minute later they started to fuss. Connie went to the room picked up Kendra and laid her beside her sister they calmed down and the family said will I will be.

Connie said the nurse's at the hospital found out that they do better together everyone stayed for a couple hours before they left for home soon it just Richard and Connie. Richard said we are going to have our hands full Connie said do not count on getting much sleep. I am glad I am bottle feeding I have no idea how to breast feed two babies at once.

The rest of the day and night went as expected Richard got up to get ready for work, both were tired Connie put on a pot of coffee while fixing breakfast. One of the twins began to fuss Richard went to check on them it turned out one lost her pacifier, he put it back in her mouth then left the room they was quiet. Cinder come over and hour

Black Rose

before Richard went to work he know sooner left when Connie began warming up bottles. Cinder told her they was to hot and showed her how to check then placing them in cold water to cool them down.

While the bottles was cooling down in the water the twins got fussing. Connie took one Cinder took the other after taking off the diaper Cinder said good reason why to fuss a wet diaper. Connie went to check on the bottles to see if they were cool enough, when got the work just before the help started to come in. they ask about the babies and he told them he was working on his third cup of coffee. Minutes before lunch Kendra began to cry Cinder said I got her Connie look on Cinder checking the diaper.

Cinder said that is a good reason to cry a messy diaper taking it off and letting some air down there while she got another diaper. When putting a fresh one on she notice Kendall's face she said oh know you don't you do not have to copy your sister. Connie got laughing then said mom I got her when she gets done look at Kendall Connie said just do not fill it up.

Richard called during lunch time to see how everything was going,Connie said she was doing good then told him about the twins Richard laughed. That evening Connie bathed one then handed her to her daddy he would diaper her then dress her. But while diapering her he went to put the diaper under her and she peed on his hand. Richard said hey that was not nice then went to get a fresh one after that he out her pajamas on her.

He filled Connie in Connie said yuck then laughed they laid both girls on a blanket on the flood until they fell asleep. Then picking them up and carrying them to there beds each in there own bed. Days turned into weeks soon it was time for Connie's six week appointment. Both Connie and the twins checked out good so Richard put her back on the schedule.

On Connie's first day back all the regular customers was welcoming her back then ask about the baby. Connie said I had twin girls they would say twins wow for Connie it was nice being back and she got tickled watching peoples face's on the reaction on there faces. Curtis came over often his first grandchildren who happen to be twins.

Between work and the twins time flew by for Richard and Connie, Kendall and Kendra were now four months old. Laying on a blanket on the floor Connie was doing dinner dishes Richard was in the living room with the girls. When he saw Kendall roll over he called Connie she came in asking what is it? Richard said look at the girls. Connie ask did you put her on her back? Richard said no Connie went to go flip her back over until she saw Kendra trying something. Then over on her back she went this surprised Connie she said I have to go finish dishes then rushed to get them done.coming back in and setting down beside Richard they end up watching the girls instead of TV. It was not much longer after when Cinder was baby setting she saw Kendra near the coffee table. Cinder ask what are you up to? She watched Kendra struggle to pull herself up. But she got up the legs a little wobbly but she was afraid to move Cinder then ask now what Kendra smiled catching her balance.

After Cinder fed them their lunch she laid them down for a nap then had her lunch. Cinder had her hour and a half of silence before both woke up making and attempt to crawl. Cinder said we are going to have fun once you two figure that out. Sunday the store was always closed Curtis and cinder went over to see Richard and Connie. Curtis was wanting to see visit his grandchildren Richard heard a knock at the door. Looking out the door window seeing his parents he said come on in then going back to the living room.

Where the twins was standing at the coffee table Curtis went over and sat down right beside them. Connie said dad you do not need to set on the floor Curtis said it is OK I want to be right beside these two. Kendall and Kendra took there first steps holding on to the coffee table with a little work they both got crawling not getting to far from each other.

Picture were taken of the twins Curtis had one in the store Richard had one in his office Connie carried one in her apron. To show the customers because some of them do ask about the twins. Now when the twins were one Curtis and Cinder went on vacation Richard and Connie joined them paying Joe to take them up there.

He had just bought his second plane and amphibious plane this was knew for everyone landing on water.

Curtis and Richard had bought some meat for the week the cabin stayed stocked of non-perishable food. Other family members use it too as long as they follow Curtis's rules he did not mind. Which was clean the cabin before you leave it and help keep it stocked bury all fish remains. They had two days left before a few other family members decided to join them for some fishing. They started early the next day stopping at three in the afternoon while the kids played. The caught enough for a fish fry some of the women began putting together some side dishes. While Curtis fire up the grill he made and cleaned a couple weeks ago.

Joe came back at a certain time to take some of them home leaving Curtis,Richard and there family to themselves. Richard sat back watching his daughters then said dad family is nice to have but this right now feels so good. Curtis said yes I have to agree nice and peaceful they both took a sip of there beer. Now as far as trash it was kept in a garbage bag and taken down with them when they leave.

Kendall and Kendra grew now Richard and Connie found themselves enrolling the girls in kindergarten. Richard and Connie both told the teacher and principal not to separate the girls. Now the school had two kindergarten rooms the third day they separated the girls, fifteen minute later both girls laid there heads down The teacher thought they was sick.

One of the teachers called Richard saying the girls are sick Richard ask where is her sister? We gave orders they are not to be separated. The teacher said we think we know best Richard said they are not your daughters we know them better then you. Kendall and Kendra are not your normal twins now listen to someone ho know them better the you. Now put them back together and let them know or I will come down with a lawyer.

When Richard hung up looking up he saw Connie standing in his office door. She said there is a client upstairs Richard said thank you then got up Connie ask what was that about? Richard said they separated the girls. Connie said didn't we tell them! Richard said yes this is why I spoke to them the way I did. When the teacher got off the phone she went to the one that had Kendra. Telling her what Richard said that teacher said they sure did say that, Bring Kendall over here Kendra has ad empty chair beside her.

They thought she was sick walking her Kendall over and setting her beside her sister. They saw each other taking each others hand until they felt better the one teacher thought Richard was out of line. So she went to speak to a child psychologist about them the doctor ask how can I help you? The teacher said we have a set of twin girls in our class five year old. The she told her about the phone conversation with Richard then ending by saying he was out of line. The doctor's name was Tari Keys Dr. keys said there are studies out where some not all twins have a bond with one another.

To where they feel each other pains even each others emotions the teacher was surprise to hear this. The teacher said we have had twins before but not like these Dr. Keys said not all twins are this way the ones that are this way are rare. The teacher said thank you to Dr. Keys I think it is time I go back to school. Then the doctor ask about their parents and the teacher told her who they was and where they worked.

The teacher went back and told her colleagues what she had learned but Tari keys she got very interested. So the next day she decide to have lunch at the BBQ pit the hostess meet her asking how many? Tari said I would like to speak to Richard Sandaro. The hostess looked around and she saw Connie who by now was the lead waitress. The hostess said his wife is right over there ma'am I can get her if you wish. Tari said sure she came back with Connie, Connie ask how can I help you? Tari said I am Dr. Tari Keys I am a child psychologist. I understand you have a set of twin girls Connie said yes what is wrong? Tari said nothing can we talk? Connie looked at the hostess asking her to take upstairs to table six.

Connie informed the waitress and found Richard who just signed off on a delivery. Together they went upstairs to talk to this doctor the hostess gave her a menu and a glass of water. By the time they got up there Tari Keys gave the waitress her order. Connie introduced Richard to Dr. Keys then they sat down Richard have you ordered.

Tari said yes I ordered the chicken dinner this is my third time here I enjoy the spicy food.

Richard ask how can we help you? Tari said I understand you have a rare set of twins. Both Richard and Connie got a weird look on there faces when she said that. Richard ask what do you mean? Tari told them about her talk with the teacher then they began to understand. As they talked the waitress brought her lunch then put the bib on her. Connie said I don't like our daughters being guinea pigs Tari said I just wish to watch them and learn there are not a lot of twins like your daughters. Richard said or she can come out to the house and study them there Connie said I will agree to that. Dr. Keys we are off in three days if you wish to study them your are welcome to come over for lunch.

Tari thought on it this was her only chance she agreed to it the they gave her their address, then told her when they would be off. Then they left Tari finished her meal when she was done she told her colleagues. When that day came Connie decided to make a casserole with garlic bread. Tari got there forty five minutes before lunch as the twins ask for their toes to be painted just like mommies. Connie told them to pick the color of mail polish out while she made the lunch. Richard answer the door and let Tari in he said welcome come on in he told Tari the girls want their toe nails painted.

Tari said Really! Richard said there is one problem with that they are very ticklish. Kendall and Kendra picked out the color then ran to the kitchen saying together mommy we found one. Connie said OK but it will have to wait until after lunch they both frowned at first then looked at each other and smiled. Then ask can daddy do it? Connie said you can ask Kendall and Kendra walked to the living room where there day was talking to Tari. When they walked in Tari ask how you tell them apart? They talked at the same time asking daddy will you do our toes? Richard ask Connie if she did anything to prep before painting her nail.

Connie said yes I put cotton in between my toes Richard said oh this will be fun Connie giggled saying yes their feet are very ticklish. Richard walked back the living Kendall and Kendra were setting on the couch. kneeling down in front of them asking for there feet as he was doing Kendra's first.

She got laughing as the cotton was place between her toes Kendall grabbed her feet. Richard said to Tari this should be fast there nails are small in minute Kendra was done. Now for Kendall she reacted the same way as her toes were being prep. With both girls toe nails done they sat there smiling as they dried. Once they was dry they took the stuff form between their toes then ran to show there mother. Tari followed them they was very excited Connie looked say cute now how about you two helping. Pointing to Kendall you get five forks then to Kendra you get five spoons together they set the table. Connie ask Tari coffee or water Tari said coffee please the twins said we will get the cups, Connie said you two stay off the counter.

Connie looked at Tari saying they will help each other to climb on the counter, Connie got the cup handing them to the girls now the table was set. Dr. Keys saw the twins did everything together and talked at the same time. During lunch Tari ask do they ever talk separately? Connie said only if the other in not in the room. Richard said you can send lets say Kendall in to go change her clothes, then blind fold Kendra. Then lets Kendra change after Kendall leaves and she will come out with the same clothes as Kendall put on.

Tari keys stuck around for a couple hours more after lunch, then thanking them for there time for allowing her to observe the girls. With this information when she went back to work she share it with her colleagues. Joe took a vacation spending a week at the cabin with his wife and son.

The cabin was a hot spot for the family to go for some peace and relaxation. When Joe was not flying he helped out at the store by unloading trucks and keeping the inventory. One day Joe found something in back he called his father showing him Curtis said that was suppose to be picked up six months ago.

Curtis called the phone number and he got a hello Curtis ask for the name on the note. A voice said I am his eldest son he was my father and he died six months ago a sudden heart attack. Curtis told him why he was calling the man said oh yes Mr. Sandaro my father

Black Rose

was looking to that but end up having a heart attack, before he could get it. Curtis ask what about what I have? The man said it is your now when they hung up he told them what he found out. Then looking at Joe asking him to take it to the cabin it will be out of sight there. Gwen said I don't recall this ever happening Jake said it never has there has always been a pick up or delivery.

Joe said I think it will look good on the stand in the dinning room the one in the corner. Curtis said that might be the only spot for it out of sight from the law. Joe said dad I will take it up there tomorrow after breakfast then do some fishing while I am up there. Curtis said that is a good place to hunt as well Jake said Charlie and I got a couple deer up there. While Richard and Connie talked about moving into a bigger place, they ended up buying a four bedroom house with fifteen acres It also had a barn. Now trying to get the girls to sleep in separate rooms now the barn the fix up for storage for the family business.

They also insulted a rope swing and a zip line inside the barn, the zip line was small but the girls enjoyed it. The also found a good spot for a garden which the family helped with, now Richard and Connie did not look over all their land. One evening they was setting outside Kendall and Kendra came running to their parent. Saying we found something Richard said OK show us what you two found. Both of them followed the girls after a little walk the girls pointed to a small building. Richard and Connie laughed a little Richard said that is and outhouse. He opened the door to show them see it is ad outside potty both girls look in with interest.

Connie said I see I am going to have to spruce it up Richard said it does look like it is good shape for it's age, then a spider came down both girls screamed Richard said he goes as well.

CHAPTER 6

Kendall and Kendra was eight years old when a man named Tony Burton, he was the head of and organized crime family in New York. He had heard about Sandaro's smuggling and was wanting to expand, so Tony and four of his men walked in to the store asking to speak to the owner.

Curtis ask how can I help you? Tony ask would you be interest in selling your store? Curtis said it is not for sale. Tony said apparently you miss understood my words I want your store, Curtis grabbed his gun and stuck it in his face. Then said I built this business now if any of your men so much as put a finger on there guns I will blow your brains out. Your not the first one to come in here making that claim as Tony back away he said your making a mistake then left.

Curtis put away his gun then looking at Gwen and Jake saying tell the family to prepare for war. Then calling Richard and filling him in on what went down Curtis ask for guards around the clock for the store. Now between the smuggling, the store and the restaurant Curtis built up a wealth of four million dollars. Richard and most of the family worked there the next couple of day some came forward for guards. Then Scott Zebulon called just to say hello to a friend Curtis said you have bad timing.

Scott ask why is that? Curtis said a Tony Burton came in wanting to buy the store, he then told him what went down. Scott said this Tony Burton is a crime boss from New York a real big wig he is worse then the one you set to prison. Curtis said just great things are running so smooth right now I also hired some family to guard the store I have a feeling he will be coming for it. Scott said what I can do is make some calls to the others you deal with sending more people to guard you. Curtis said thank you but what will this cost me? Scott said nothing my friend if he gets your store we will not like how he deal he is bad news.

Curtis said I am telling anyone using a shot gun to replace the buck shot with metal shaving. Scott said playing a little dirty are we Curtis said just sending a message. When they hung up Scott began calling the others to tell them what is going down. No one like tony Burton and they had heard how he deals so they was more then willing to send Curtis some men. With in two weeks Curtis had plenty of men to guard the store, Richard and some of his family the employees began to pack as well. They was ready the waitresses and both hostess hid guns in there aprons.

Curtis was ready when two men walked in the store one side MR. Burton wants to know if you reconsidered his offer? Curtis said my answer is still no one of the men said things might break in your store. Just then a hammer came back on a gun and a a voice said you break it you bought it, the two men turned there heads slowly to see a gun. The two men turned to Curtis which had a gun pointing at them, they held their hands out and said we will give our boss your answer then they left slowly .

They went back to Tony and told him what went down Tony said he is stronger then I thought. The law cannot seem to catch him I want that business, the guards for the store sat in their cars in the parking lot. Curtis would buy there lunch as they went to the restaurant across the street.

A week went by when they saw a car coming down the road, as they saw both passenger windows come down they went on alert. Then they saw guns come out as gun fire was exchanged everyone in the store hit the floor. As the car reached the far end of the parking lot someone fired a double barrel shot gun loaded with what Curtis ask for.

The restaurant called the police as the car drove off, there was a couple inside shopping at the time the man was wounded One dead in the car that drove by. A few wounded and a window shot out in the store the police came four cars altogether. Once the police found out what happened they spread out taking reports from I witness one witness in the restaurant parking lot got the license plate number.

The last person they talked to was Curtis and the others working inside the store. This is where they found out Tony Burton was in town and that he wanted Sandaro's Trading. They knew Tony Burton was a crime boss with urgency they report it to there captain. He in turn went to the chief of police he said oh great this is something we do not need. He went on tell the men to hit the streets to see if we can find him after the captain left. The chief called the chief of police in New York he introduced him self and his town and state.

The New York chief of police said what is the pleasure of your called sir? The other chief of police said we have one of your people here. New York chief of police ask who may that be? The other said Tony Burton! The New York chief took notice on that name then ask what is he doing there? The other police chief said causing trouble. He is trying to take over a store that has been in business for nearly thirty years. The new York chief ask how is the owner taking it? The other chief said he just had a gun fight with him they just did a drive by.

The new York police chief said he is on the feds most wanted list thank you for the information. When they hung up the New York chief police called the Feds telling them what Tony Burton has been up to. The Feds took that information and left for that town pulling up to the police station going straight to the captain.

Flashing him their ID's then said we want everything on Tony Burton you have the case is now ours. Just then a knock at the captain's door a officer said captain we found the car in the drive by. A Federal agent said have the car towed to the impounded meant lot. The office ask who are you? The agent showed him his ID then said anything on Tony Burton comes to us.

When they saw the car it had bullet holes all over the passenger side, the front window shattered blood on the seats along with a few bullet casing. They was very thorough searching the car writing down everything they found. By the time they was done it was late they had many finger prints, the next day they ran the prints. Everyone was Burton's men. Then they rode to Sandaro's Trading and interviewed everyone there.

Just as they was about to get in there cars they looked around one agent said where this store is at, it would be a prefect spot. From there they went to town and began asking around showing a picture of Tony Burton. Burton tried again this time he sent two men at night to set the store on fire. The used a Molotov cocktail they pulled in the edge of the parking lot as soon as he lite it a shot rang out. Hitting the man in the side dropping the bottle it broke igniting some of his clothes.

Putting out the fire he ran to the car holding his side the driver took off fast taking him straight to the emergency room. The next morning the Feds got a phone call telling them about the man Burton was upset when his third try failed. Tony did admire Curtis Sandaro on how he handled things, this told him why he had been in business for so long. By the time Feds got to the hospital to talk to this man he had escaped.

Curtis was filled in on what happened that night then ask of anyone was hurt? The person that told him smiled then said only the person trying to burn the store. Tony was none to happy one of his men said boss source's say that his Curtis Sandaro has a big smuggling ring going on here. Tony ask then why has not the police caught him? One of his men said that is just it they have been in his store a few times and found nothing. Tony said what is that saying? You want to hide something stick it under there nose.

Looking at his men he said ice him four men left watching the store at a distance. Curtis left for the evening to go deposit the money it seemed the bank parking lot was always busy at this time. Rolling down their windows for a drive by the federal agents just walk out a business, they saw Curtis another agent spotted the car. He saw the gun the said they are going for him as the car drove up the federal agent opened fired on the car. Wounding one of the men the car drove off fast Curtis stopped to see what was going on.

The agent told Curtis the drive by was meant for him Curtis said I will not hide. The agent said we have been after him for years Curtis said one thing people with to much conference. They do not pay attention to the little mistakes they make then Curtis went inside to deposit the money for the day. His men dump the car at a chop shop paying the manager to make it disappear. Not knowing these was some of Curtis's customers when the men left they called Brain Metzlor. Telling him about the car dropped off with bullet holes Brain aid set it aside I will look at in it the morning.

The next morning Brain called Curtis about the car Curtis smiled saying that was a mistake. Brain said mistake! What do you mean? Curtis said that car was part of a foiled drive by. Brain ask who was they trying to hit? Curtis said me but the Feds messed it up while he was looking at it a patrol car scouting the neighborhood. When they saw Brain and the car the ran the plates turning around once they found out it was wanted by the feds. Then asking Brain where did he get it? Brain said one of my workers said some men dropped it off last night. One of the officers said that car is wanted by the feds in a drive by shooting.

Brain ask anyone got killed? The officer said no they got a couple shots off but missed, the car was towed and kept quiet then dusted for prints. All prints matched Tony's men with some blood stains telling them one was hit. So they began checking all the hospitals to see if anyone came in with a bullet wound.

Mean while Tony found out that Curtis Sandaro owned the restaurant called the BBQ pit and he had three kids. So Tony sent a man over to make sure the BBQ pit catches fire the mans name was Cordell Thomas. He walked through the doors of the restaurant the hostess stopped him asking him can I help you? Cordell said I was called to do some repairs here.

The hostess said wait here please she went and got Richard. He came out asking may I help you? Cordell said I am here to do some repairs sir . Richard said I do not know anything about repairs! Cordell said well sir I got a call Richard said sir I am the manager I would be the first person to know about any repairs. I am going to ask you to leave and if you do not I will interrupt those police officers over there having there lunch to escort you out. And if that is not enough most of my employees do have some heat on them. Cordell turned and left he did not want to cause a scene he called Tony when he got back to his apartment.

Tony Burton sat and thought he was not getting anywhere, he was not counting on Curtis being this strong then again you have to be doing what he does. Tony did some further investigating and found out that Richard the manager of the BBQ pit was Curtis's son. He told a couple of his men to learn what he could about him, a couple days later they came back Richard Sandaro owns two house's and rent out one the other is out in the country. He also has two daughters who are twins and manages the the BBQ pit rumors has it this is where they meet the clients at.

The second house he has sets out in the country on fifteen acres Tony thought then said have everyone here in two days. What Tony did not know was that Richard was off in two days Tony's men gathered he said we are going to put Richard Sandaro in ice. That should force Curtis Sandaro to sell me his store so I can have that smuggling business.

It was a Saturday both Richard and Connie were off, Connie was getting breakfast as the twins was getting up sleeping in the same bed. When they had bedrooms of their own Connie and Richard could not figure it out. Richard helped Connie with breakfast and dishes then told her he had to go to the hardware store.

The twins was nine Kendall ask to go with him Richard said OK lets go, now the hardware store was a nice little drive. Tony and his men spotted Richard leaving the hardware store then followed. Both cars got on a stretch of road where no cars or house's were Tony told his men pass him up they sped past him. They found the prefect spot then blocked the road forcing Richard to stop when he got to them. Kendall ask daddy who is that man? Richard said his name is Tony Burton. Tony walked up to Richard's car surprised to see a little girl asking are you Richard Sandaro? Richard said yes I am.

Reaching behind him pulling a gun out shooting Richard twice then going around and beating Kendall then trying to put her eyes out. Kendra was watching TV Connie was getting another cup of coffee when Kendra screamed a blood curling scream. Connie ran in to where she was asking what is wrong Kendra said Kendall is hurting I can not see.

Connie never saw Kendra like this so she called her father in law Curtis. He was relaxing at home Gwen was there along with Joe, Jake and charlie they was all there visiting. His phone rang Curtis said hello Connie said dad please go find Richard Kendra said Kendall is hurting. Curtis ask do you know where he is? Connie said he went to the hardware store he might have taken this road naming the road. Wen he hung up he said Joe,Jake and charlie lets go Jake ask where are we going? Curtis said to find Richard that was Connie she said Kendra is going nuts saying Kendall is hurting.

Joe said maybe he got in and accident Curtis said we are heading to the old state road. They took two separate cars they went to the old state road driving along when they spotted Richard's car. Pulling over they ran to the car shocked to see the sight Curtis saw Kendall opening the door she had been beaten. He touched her she screamed Curtis said it is grandpa repeating it until she calmed down.

Then he took her in his arms and said someone find a phone Joe said I have a friend in the area jumping in his car and raced off. Curtis said Burton is dead Joe got to his friend's in know time knocking on the door. Pete his friend said hey Joe what is up? Joe said I need to use your phone! Pete saw his face it was not good. Pete let him in Joe called the police the dispatcher answer Joe said I need the police and life squad out on old state road right before the bend.

The dispatcher ask may I know why? Joe said we just found my brother shot and my niece had been beaten please hurry. As Joe hung up Pete stared at him asking when? Joe said with in the last forty five minutes Joe said thank you for the phone then left. The police and life squad finally got there they saw Curtis holding a little girl. As the life squad checked out Richard the police ask Jake who are you? Jake pointing to Richard saying I am his cousin. his father is the one holding the girl which is his granddaughter.

The paramedics pronounced Richard dead they then went to Kendall Curtis said she is alive and I am going with her. The police took reports from everyone then ask do you know who did this? Curtis said Tony Burton. Looking at Joe and the rest you three go tell the family I am going with Kendall. Joe, Jake and charlie looked at each other this is news they will not take pleasure in delivering. Joe went to his mother's house the other two went to tell Connie tears coming down their faces. Joe told both women the shock hit them then the tear flowed, Jake and charlie told Connie.

Kendra ask about her sister Charlie told her she at the hospital with grandpa Richard had taken out life insurance on both of them after they got married. Connie ask to be taken to the hospital they then joined Curtis in the waiting room, some time went by when a doctor came out. The doctor was surprised to see Kendra Connie said this is her twins sister they never been separated until now and she is going nuts.

The doctor saw the stress on Kendra's face then said to the family I am putting her in ICU for now. As for her sight who ever did this did a bad job if she stays like this she will be blind. I think surgery might restore some of her sight I know a specialist who is very good with this kind of thing. Kendra ask can I see my sister she is hurting the doctor said you are to young. Kendra said please she is hurting! Connie said this is her twin sister they can feel each others emotion, The doctor has never experienced anything like this.

The doctor went and called that specialist telling him about Kendall. He came as fast as he could after seeing her he ask what happened? As he looked over her eyes DR. Lark told him. The specialist who's name was Dr. Parson, Dr. Lark said she does have a twin sister that says she is hurting. Dr. Parson said that is no surprise when it comes to twins Dr. Lark what do you mean? Dr. Parson said some twins not all have this unusual connection.

They feel each others pain and emotions if this is the case here you might have to call her in. Dr. lark ask what is your thought? Dr. Parson said if she stays this way she will be blind for life. Surgery will help the sooner the better Dr. lark said we can do it now I have a crew on stand by, her grandmother is in the waiting room. Connie had just arrived with Joe Dr. Lark went to get thing ready while Dr. Parson went to tell the family. So while Kendall was gong into surgery Cinder, Connie and Joe went to the funeral home to plan Richards funeral.

Curtis was on the phone calling all his business partners for a meeting at the BBQ pit. Then telling them why the meeting was in seven days Cinder called Curtis giving him and update he was at the store. He then went to open the BBQ pit some employees did not know Richard always help and opening meeting. When the was all there Curtis stood up saying if you have not heard Richard was killed yesterday. I am placing Connie in his spot she and Cinder are making funeral arrangements as we speak. Kendall their daughter is going for emergency surgery as the meeting ended the phone rang.

Curtis answered the phone the BBQ pit, Tony Burton said you still refuse to sell me your store. Curtis said you son of a bitch I will kill you! Tony said who do you think your talking to? Curtis said you are a pile of shit I do not care who you are. I will blow your head off and if I see any one of your men they are dead men walking you are not in New York.

Curtis called the fill in manager to step in until Conner was ready then he went to the hospital, where he would meet up with his wife and Conner. The surgery was a success Dr. Parson told the family she should between 60 -80 percent of her eye sight back, She will be kept in ICU for another day then moved to her own room.

When they moved her to her own room family began to come and stay twenty four seven. The third in her room a nurse came to check on

Kendall then after words told Cinder she should be improving. Cinder said she needs her sister we told them that, the next day Connie was working a waitress ask her what are you doing here? Connie said I need a distraction or I am going to lose it. Dr. lark called Connie Cinder told him where to find her the hostess called Connie to the phone. Connie said hello the voice said this is Dr. lark Kendall is not getting better I am going to break protocol.

I would like you to bring her sister in maybe it might help turn thing around. Connie called the fill in manager as soon as he got there she told him what was up and left. Kendra lucky it was summer break her sister was watching Kendra calling her sister and asking her to tell Kendra to be ready when she got there. As soon as she pulled in the driveway Kendra got in asking where are we going? Connie said the doctor is breaking the rules and letting you see your sister.

They got the the hospital in know time as they entered her room Kendra saw her grandmother. She froze for a minute when she saw her sister walking to her side of the bed Cinder said on this side she has and IV in that arm. She went to the other side taking her hand and saying I am her now Connie picked her up placing her by her side on the bed.

Then Kendall's mind snapped to a time when she was being beaten, Kendra said no he cannot hurt you any more I am here she was squeezing her hand. Kendall calmed down then a few hours later Cinder went home to fix dinner saying I will send both of you something back Connie said thank you mom. She left and a nurse came in saying you two will have to leave while I check on her.

Kendra began to tear up the nurse said sweetie you can come back in a few minutes as soon as I am done this will take just a couple minutes I promise. While checking on Kendall she found that Kendall was improving this surprised her. When she was done she let Connie and Kendra back in then went and told the RN. Cinder just walked through the door when the phone rang she answer it, it was her son Joe. He was telling her how Tammy his wife and him was going up to see Kendall and that her mother was watching the kids. Cinder said do me a favor take Connie and Kendra up some food Joe said sure no problem. Joe and Tammy stopped by a near by restaurant to eat then ordered a take out for two to go.

Tammy handed them there dinner Joe ask how is Kendall doing? Kendra said she is starting to feel better. This caught Joe off guard he looked at Kendra asking her how do you do that? He had a puzzled looked oh his face. Kendra giggled saying we just know they stayed for a couple hours before they left. That evening Connie slept in a chair Kendra laid down by her sister around midnight a nurse came in to check on Kendall. She thought it was so cute seeing the twins sleeping together until she saw Kendall arm around Kendra. This shocked her she rushed to the nurse's station asking the RN to follow her I want you to see this. The nurse said looked at the patience's arm the RN said that is a good sign I will make sure breakfast is brought in to her.

The nurse woke Connie saying I need to check on Kendall Connie woke Kendra as the nurse was checking on her she saw her arm slowly move. The nurse said she will be back in a couple minutes after writing on her chart the nurse told them they could go back in. Kendall settled back down when she felt her sister Cinder and Curtis came in the room bringing them breakfast. Kendra was laying there awake the smell of food was strong Kendall whispered I am hungry. Kendra said I will share my breakfast with you. Kendra lifted up her head as she sat up they saw Kendall's arm move everyone was smiling.

Cinder handed Kendra some pancakes Kendra thanked her after the syrup was poured on them she ask Kendall to open up. Cutting off a piece then putting in her mouth then she took a bite. The doctor stopped by the nurse's station and was informed about Kendall so he went in to see Kendra was feeding her. The doctor said I do not understand the connection but I like the results. The doctor ask Kendall how she was feeling after swallowing her food she said I am sore but good, he noticed her hand was on her sister.

Connie said when they are done Kendra and I are going home to bath, Kendra gave her a sharp look. Connie said if you don't bath the hospital will chase you out because you stink. Kendall got laughing waving her hand in front of her nose Kendra said very funny. Kendall

Black Rose

ask her to bring back a sandwich and they said pig skins together, the doctor said they have breakfast coming for you Kendall smiled.

Connie and Kendra left soon the doctor ask nurse to bring in fresh bandages he was wanting to check her eyes. Curtis and Cinder stepped out of the room it was over a week sense her eye operation. The doctor was wanting to see how things were doing then brought then in Dr. Lark ask Kendall to close her eyes. Taking off the bandages Kendall slowly opened them then suddenly closed them.

Dr. Lark ask what is wrong? Kendall said the light hurts my eyes Dr. lark said them are the ceiling lights. She opened eyes again slowly Dr. Lark looked at them then said they are coming along just find. He then place fresh bandages back over her eyes, back home Kendra bath first then Connie. But while she was bathing Kendra made her sister a sandwich bologna, cheese mayonnaise and a pickle cut In four pieces.

When Connie was dressed she ask Kendra ready? Kendra held up a plastic bag with the sandwich saying mom don't forget the pig skins. They got in the car and drove to the BBQ pit Connie and Kendra sat at the counter asking the waitress for a bag of pork rinds. The waitress ask what size Connie looking at Kendra then said make that a large bag. The waitress ask Kendra you eating them by yourself? Kendra said no Kendall is helping looking at Connie saying she is awake! Connie smile saying yes she woke up this morning.

When they got back to the hospital Kendra was rushing Connie said slowly your in the hospital. Kendra said hi grandpa and grandma then she waved the bag under Kendall's nose and giggled. Kendall ask some help me set up Kendra sat on the bed as she shared the Cajun pork rinds with her sister then sandwich Kendall ate slow. Everyone there was smiling watching both girls eat together when Kendall was done she let out a loud burp. Cinder said my word I hope the nurse did not hear that Curtis laughed a week went by Kendall improved a lot. Curtis, Jake and Charlie came in the room Kendall always had four to five family members in the room.

The people Curtis had called started to arrive asking to speak to rose these guest was escorted upstairs. Each one expressed there condolences about Richard then they sat down. when everyone was there Curtis said welcome gentlemen help yourself to what is on the table. You know why we are here we ave a rat in the house one of the men said yes a big rat too making waves at our end as well.

Curtis said I have a feeling the feds are waiting for my granddaughter to be well enough to talk to. One of the group said we should try and find more witnesses another said they will be afraid to talk with someone as powerful as Tony Burton is. Curtis said what if we hid them? They all looked at each other one from the group said Burton's men will be watching the feds. One from the group said what if someone take out Burton? Curtis said I will give him a half I million. Another one said hey guys why don't we meet his part there was ten men there, they all agree and the contract was made.

Two hours later three federal agents walked in to Kendall's room by then Curtis and Connie was there. Curtis saw them then said I was wondering how long it would take for you all to get here. One of the agent said I am sorry she is are only witness Curtis introduced them to Connie she ask can I help you? And agent said we need to talk to Kendall Sandaro. Connie said she is a child and agent said she is the only witness to the murder of your husband.

Connie explained to Kendall why the men were here she squeezed Kendra's hand, Kendra said he cannot hurt you he cannot hurt mom or grandpa. Then the men ask her we do not wish to put you through this but can you remember what happened? She slowly told her story. While she was doing that two men appeared at her door Charlie saw them he knew who they were. Walking over he ask everything OK? One of the men smiled and said we found three witnesses.

Charlie said that is great see those men over there, they are the feds. They are talking a statement from Kendall one of the men said that is not right Charlie said she is all they have. Why not work out a deal while they are here Charlie called Curtis over. When Kendall was done the Feds said we have him then thanking Kendall for her statement.

Curtis said see those men over there they found three other witnesses. The agents walked over to them asking we hear you have witnesses one of the men said yes we found three they are willing

Black Rose

to testify. They know Tony Burton Iced Richard Sandaro and agent said we want statements and put them under protection. One of the men said one thing about that you feds keep losing witnesses when it comes to Burton.

Here is our deal we get immunity and we keep the witnesses until court date. The Feds did not like the deal, one of the men said like we said you Feds keeps losing people trying to get Burton. Once they make there statement his men will follow you around like a lost dog trying to get them. One agent said but he will not suspect you are keeping them another agent said I do not like the deal but if it is to Get Tony Burton you have a deal.

Another ask can you get them to this address one of the men said yes tomorrow. As the agents left to get and arrest warrant the men walked in the room. Asking how Kendall was Connie said she is doing good they are talking about her releasing her. The Sandaro's knew the men one of the men said to Kendall you do not worry sweetie we are watching over you.

Two hours later the agents had there warrant then forty five minutes later after they found Tony Burton they arrested him for the murder of Richard Sandaro. Later that day Connie was watching TV in Kendall's room on the evening news it said earlier today the crime Boss Tony Burton was arrested for the murder of Richard Sandaro. The next day at one they brought the witnesses in to the federal agents after they gave there statements they disappeared Until the court date.

A week later they let Kendall go home with and appointment to see Dr Parson in two weeks. Connie returned to work and Cinder took Kendall to her appointment . Taking off her bandages her eyes looked good then they examined her for glasses. Dr. Parson said her glasses would be in in two weeks Cinder took both girls out to lunch at the BBQ pit. Kendra had Kendall's hand. They eye doctor said she had eighty percent of her eye sight. When they walked in everyone was so happy to see Kendall most of them gave her a big hug. The girls said hi to there mother before being taken to there booth. That is when Kendall said she had to use the bathroom with her eye sight not that great Kendra took her hand.

Kendall came out holding her nose Kendra said that bad! They called the waitress at the counter to report the smell. She walked in coming out said be right back asking Connie for some spray. Saying the ladies room smells bad and the twins are waiting, she sprayed down the restroom then said now try it. Up on getting her glasses now she was smiling because she could see good now.

Then Connie took then school shopping Gwen, Heather and Cinder went with her School was a week away. Gwen said to the twins I want to try something with you two, now Kendall I want you to go with Grandma and Heather and pick out what you want but do not show your sister. Kendra you do the same thing they ask why Gwen said I want to see if you two will pick out the same thing or something different.

When both girl went shopping and they when they was in car they took out their clothes they got. Both ended up getting the same thing as the other Heather said I cannot believe this. The court date came around Kendra had to go to school she told her sister to be strong make him pay what he did to our daddy. Remember mommy and grandpa will be with you, people poured in the court room and the three witnesses arrived.

Tony Burton was setting there when he saw Kendall walk in with Curtis and a woman, he looked at her like he saw a ghost. He thought he killed her Curtis gave him a dirty look the prosecutor looked around all his witnesses were here. As the court began the first three witnesses was called they was cross examined. Kendall was last after she was worn in the prosecutor ask her to try and recall that day. She told hr story and was not cross examined then the prosecutor entered the pictures of Kendall. What the police took of her that day the jury was released to vote they came back after and hour. Saying we the jury find Tony Burton guilty of first degree murder they also found him guilty on all charges against Kendall. The judge gave him the maxim sentence making sure he never saw the outside of a prison.

CHAPTER

7

Four months had past the twins were nine now all the children in the family was watching over the twins in school. Gwen had called the BBQ pit to order there lunch, Curtis and Jake was going after it. When they got there Curtis said to Jake you get the lunch ready I am going to go check on Connie he found her in the office. Eating lunch and looking at some paper work Curtis said you don't work and have lunch at the same time. Connie jumped swallowing what she was chewing on saying oh dad hi Curtis ask how are you? Connie said I am good but her face told the truth Curtis said we all miss him your not alone.

   Curtis sat down Connie ask what brings you here? Curtis said we ordered lunch. Connie said I was thinking of putting the girls in marshal arts Curtis said I might be able to help with that. I heard of a hit man that is laying low he does most of his jobs with his hands rumor has it he is and eighth degree black belt. Connie said you want a hit man to train my girl! Curtis said well he is laying low and he is and expert in marshal arts. Connie said I can not believe you then smiled Curtis ask OK what is cooking in that brain of yours? Connie

Black Rose

said if he will train them in everything he does. When they get old enough I can remind them who killed there father and cut them lose.

Curtis ask around with his contacts and they found the hit man trying to lay low. Logan Aaron wan his name he was one of the top hit men he had been busy with contracts and a lot was done with his hands. He got word someone was wanting a teacher he began to ask around, it lead him to Sandaro's General store walking in he saw Gwen at the counter. Logan ask is there a Curtis or Connie Sandaro here? Gwen said Curtis is my father he is in the middle of unloading a truck. Connie works at the BBQ pit if you go there ask for rose Logan ask her where this place was at she told him.

He said thank you then left for the BBQ pit the hostess ask him how many sir? Logan said I would like to speak to rose. The hostess said this way sir taking him up stairs and setting him at a table giving him a menu then saying someone will be right with you. Then she went down and told Connie handing her she said make sure the waitress knows about him. Connie went upstairs asking can I help you sir Logan said looking up from his menu. I heard someone is looking for a marshal arts teacher! Connie said that would be me for my daughters. Logan introduced himself Connie said I have heard you have been around .

One the top assassins in the world Logan smiled a little then said I see you have been doing your homework, your last name sounds familiar. Connie said Richard Sandaro was my husband Logan remembered from TV then said sorry about your husband ma'am. So you want me to teacher your daughters, Connie say yes here is something the news did not say. Tony Burton nearly beat and eight year old to death and come close to blinding her for life.

Logan said I will teach them but I have and occupation Connie said I understand, but I think you should meet them first. We are having a picnic this Saturday Logan said OK I will there she then gave him the address. A few days later Logan showed up pulling in the driveway Charlie saw him asking can I help you? Logan said I am here to see Connie Sandaro I am Logan Aaron.

Charlie said I will get her for you sir would you like a beer? They walked around back where the rest was. Walking over to Connie Charlie said this gentleman ask to see you Connie said Mr. Aaron come and see my twins, they are playing in the barn. See my late husband put up swings and a zip line inside the barn and the kids have a ball.

As soon as they opened the door Connie saw Kendra riding the zip line upside down and someone was there to catch her. Connie gasp then said oh my gosh when Kendra got off Connie said Kendra ride it the right way. Kendra said mommy you should try it, it is fun. Connie was shaking her head saying oh dear Logan said I see they like taking risk! Connie said yes and it scares the hell out of me.

Connie said to Kendra get your sister and please come here Kendra said let me use the bathroom first then ran to the back door of the barn Kendall was right behind her. Connie said to Logan the door leads to and outhouse my late husband refurbished when we bought this place. The suddenly the twins ran back inside to there mother saying there is a spider in the outhouse. Connie said oh good grief then said to Logan I will be right back Logan said allow me please. Then asking the girl to take him to the spider they took him the the outhouse opening the door slowly Kendall pointed to it both ran.

Logan noticed they was afraid of it he got a stick with a little work got the spider on it. Then he carried it away some distance then let it go. As he walked back he saw they was handing each others hand he told them it was safe. Both looked in then at each other Kendra went in shutting the door Logan went back inside. Where he ask Connie are they ever separate? Connie said no they are always in the same room together. Then they joined the rest outside Logan ask are all these people family? Most are family some are friends and business associates. He looked around some of these friends and associates was not law abiding he smiled his type of people.

The twins came out of the barn heading towards the food Connie said Kendall and Kendra are watched by all family even at school. Sense Tony Burton almost beat her to death even some business associates have her back. After the picnic Logan went to find himself and apartment Monday he would began teaching the girls. After dinner for two hours three days a week days turned into weeks, weeks turned into months, Months turn into years. Connie was always there watching Kendall and Kendra was now twelve .

Logan began training with weapons the marshal arts helped Kendra on her nightmares . Kendra could not get the throwing spikes Kendall said remember what he did to daddy. Connie and Logan was surprised by that remark Kendra concentrated then began to stick it, both girls got excited as they hit the target every time. There was a couple time Kendra flipped out during a lesson and attack Logan hard. Logan tried to stopped her Kendall ran up and said no he is not the bad guy. When she stopped Kendra fell to the floor and cried Kendall put her arms around her along with Connie.

Logan sat down with them when Kendra was calm down she told Logan she was sorry. Logan ask if she was OK Kendra said yes they continued was the lesson. On he next class Logan walked in the barn and saw both having a ball with the throwing knives, spikes and stars. Hitting the bulls eye every time then he called out hey girl class they had class for and hour and a half working with swords and staffs.

Logan in between teaching the twins did contracts, how ever he was enjoying the teaching part. He had been a loner sense his parents was killed in a car accident when he was sixteen. This brought a side of him he did not know he had in which he was enjoying. When Kendall and Kendra turned thirteen Logan began to teach them about guns.

Now guns was no stranger to the twins the Sandaro's where hunters they grew up with them. Kendall and Kendra knew the cabin as a vacation spot which they enjoyed it was also a hunting cabin as well. They target practiced behind the barn like the rest of the family it got to a point when some of the family came to target practice. The twins would ask if they could shoot their guns the girl learned to shoot 22 rifle and 410's.

Over time they got good and thought it fun so Logan thought to show them his rifle, it was a professional snipers rifle the twins thought it interesting. The he showed them how to put in together they never saw a gun like this before. Then they ask to shoot it being three month away of turning fourteen. Often during the girls spare time you would find them on the floor doing a word search together.

On there fourteenth birthday they ask for there own guns they ask for 22 automatics with silencers. so Connie spoke to Curtis telling him what the girls ask for also explaining there interest with Logan's rifle. Curtis said they are good shots and was thought how to handle a gun safely. How are you on guns with the girls? Connie said I still have Richards guns. They have started to shot them Connie giggled then said Kendra was knocked on her butt with the shot gun. The look on Kendall's face was priceless Jake and Charlie was with them as I laughed.

Curtis ask so you would not mind if I got them guns? Connie said no so Curtis went through his contacts. And not got them the guns they was asking for but also a pair of sniper rifles. It took a couple of months to find the rifles when the pistols came in he delivered in person. Kendall and Kendra was over joyed to get the pistols then ask grandpa to take them out back to shoot.

Upon there fifteen birthday they was given the rifles then they began working part time one at the store the other at the BBQ pit. So between school, marshal arts and school they stayed busy they also made sure to target practice with there guns. They was also asking around about Tony Burton people on some of there free time then Kendra said to Kendall said to her sister then we start making them pay.

Kendall said we can lay a black rose on everyone we take out, they smiled at each other. They found out that Scott Burton Tony Burton's youngest son along with a few men had moved in to that house that Tony bought years ago. so the twins began to plan to take him out they found out one of his top henchmen was going to a music festival in the summer of their sixteenth birthday.

By the time school was out for the summer the girls found out the top henchman was going to be there. It was going to take place June 28th Logan came out like normal for there class. Found them planning something he ask what are you two up to? They first looked at each other then kept silent.

Logan said I have known both of you way to long you too are up to something. The twins broke down and told him there plan to start striking back at the Burton organization. They explained there first strike showing the picture of the one they was gong after. Logan questioned them during class getting and idea how they was going to do it. How they explained the plan sounded like it might work he said I want to go with you two. They ask why? Logan said so I can watch to see if you learned anything I was trying to tech you.

The day of the music festival came the twins went to their rooms each put on a different wig. Fake eyelashes and make up Kendra put on a fake nose coming out of there rooms and looking at each other in disgust then they giggled. Then going down stairs to show their mother and Logan Connie could barely recognize her daughters both laughing at the reaction.

Each had a large bag where they had a change of clothes with and pocket inside where the kept there guns. Both had a black rose inside as well Logan ask you both ready he knew they had there own language. They set out arriving near the start of it, taking some time they found there mark. They used there own language to tell what each other was doing Logan was amazed he never saw them use it.

The music was loud as they was closing in on him the man got up, they followed him to the men bathroom. Kendall put on some sun glasses then pulled out a cane for the blind walking up to the bathroom acting like she went into the wrong one. A man said miss your in the wrong one Kendra saw no one else was in here. Pulling out her gun shooting him twice Kendall rush in as soon as she could said it was good then laid a black rose on the body then rushing in the ladies room and changing. coming out they both looked the same Kendra had put contact in which was a little surprise.

They slowly walked away ten minutes later the body was found the three walked out slowly and got in there car, Then left before the police was called. stopping along the way home at a restaurant to eat when getting home they put up there stuff then came back to watch TV. When the news came on they was all attentive hearing about a murder at the music festival with a black rose on him.

Now during the summer both girls worked full time then filling each other in at days end on what they found out. They got excited when they got information on Scott Burton Kendall showed Kendra a picture saying this is Scott Burton. He ride a motorcycle Kendra said he comes to the restaurant to eat and has a brown car Kendall said yes he always has two men with him.

Kendall said I hear he likes to ride on deer run road Kendra ask isn't that near some woods? Kendall said yes a lot of deer hunters are there. Kendra said lets go check that road and woods out Kendall smiled but before they did that they followed Scott Burton around during thee free time. They did this for a week then Logan saw them he got wondering what they was up to.

It took him a few minute but he figured it out then they stopped and went to work. So during marshal arts class that evening Logan ask them what they was up to. The twins told him then said they have to check out some woods he likes to ride his bike by. Logan ask to tag along both said they did not mind and school was just weeks away.

When class was over they told Logan they was doing it in the morning after breakfast. After dishes they called Logan telling him they was on there way, they parked where the deer hunters park. Then began to look around they explained how Scott would becoming down the rode. The three looked the area over Logan found a deer stand a few feet inside the woods.

Out of no where four deer came by startling him Logan called the girls over to show them the deer stand. It was a two man stand they went up finding a window towards the road they smiled at each other. Coming down they told Logan there plain they would barrow Jake's walkies talkies they get out as far as a mile. Kendall would let Kendra know when he was with in a mile then stay back until Kendra calls back, Logan said Kendall is doing it this time.

Kendra said no she did it last time this one is mine Logan thought to him self they had everything planned out. It was thee day off Kendra was dropped off at the deer stand it had not rained in three weeks the ground was dry. Climbing up the stand she got ready while Kendall went to find Scott which did not take long he was on his motorcycle. She smiled this time he was not wearing a helmet he left for deer run road.

As soon as they was with in a mile Kendall called over the walkie talkies, saying pretty boy is on his way Wearing no head gear. Kendra soon heard him coming she got ready aiming carefully here he came. She shot hitting him in the chest Kendra called come and get me Kendra picked up the shell casing leaving nothing behind then left. Going out where the deer hunter park as Kendra checked the body Kendall turned around the car. Kendra jumping in the back so she could break down her rifle and put it up she said he killed our father we will take what he loves.

On the way home Kendall and Kendra stopped by the BBQ pit to eat. Kendall said before they got out wait let me put my contacts in smiling as they walked in the hostess said to them you two are not right. She gave them a both then they saw there grandparents walked in with some cousins, one of the cousins said look over there. Cinder said oh look Kendall is not wearing her glasses Connie said I forgot she has contacts the cousin ask who is who? The twins laid low doing what sixteen years old do. They had a few friend over from school then they found out Tony Burton had two more Kids.

So they began asking around for information on them by he end of January they had everything on them a boy and a girl . Doug was the boys name Charlotte was the girls Doug enjoyed their vacation home built next to a large hill next to a cliff a nice view of the ocean. They got the address for that then they found out when Doug was going to be there.

They found out Charlotte was going to Paris both girls did not like this they would have to separate. through contacts they got pictures of the house and noticed the hill, they talked about shooting him from the hill then leaving on a hand glider. By the end of school everything was set what each would do along with their contacts. The time came each giving each other a big hug before setting out Kendall had taken some hand glider lessons . She went to her uncle Joe's house asking him if he could take her to this address in California.

Joe said just happen to buy a twins engine plane that will be one way to try it out. Kendall said thank you to him then said I need to see grandpa Joe ask for what? Kendall said to see if he can find a place for me to stay out there. I could rent a hotel but I do not know how long I will be Kendra was out planning her trip to Paris. The next day Kendall went to her grandfather telling him what she needed. Curtis took her in back so they could talk without the customers hearing Curtis said I will see what I can do Tony Burton has not paid enough.

Curtis got on the phone made three calls asking his contacts if they knew a place near the address he gave them. Has contact ask why? Curtis said the black Rose has business out there. There was a few minutes of silence then his contact said the Black Rose has a mark! Curtis said yes. Two weeks later Curtis got a call saying I have a place for the Black Rose to stay. Curtis said thank you my son will be flying the Black Rose out there if you would tell your family out there when it comes to the Black Rose looks are deceiving.

The twins would be leaving at the same time Kendra would go to Paris after Charlotte. The underground would be helping her with all her needs both girl were fluent in Spanish and French which helped the family business. Joe and Kendall flew out to California where a ranch owner picked them up. It turned out Joe knew him his name was Don Reynolds Don smiles saying Joe if I knew it was going to be you and who is this? Kendall my name is Rose. Don looked surprised looking at Joe then said you father said when it comes to the Black Rose looks are deceiving.

I was not expecting someone so young Joe smiled then said that give her and edge, Once at the ranch Don showed them the guest house. Now don's wife was from Mexico her name was Maria Don ask Joe are you two hungry? Joe said we ate this morning. Don said I will ask my wife to fix you a lunch so you can eat with us, Don also had three children two daughters one son.

Brain was his son's name when Brain smiled at his bad asking who is this pretty girl? Don said her name is Rose do not get to close. Brain looked at his dad asking why not? Don said she is also called the black Rose and she is here on business now where is your mother? As Brain

Black Rose

watch them put there stuff up. Kendall teased her uncle asking him do you snore? Joe said no! Kendall said aunt Millie said you could shake the windows. Joe said did she now come lets fins Don if I remember his wife should be fixing lunch. On the way to the house Kendall ask do you know this man? Joe said yes I have been moving stuff for him for a few years now.

Brain opened the door for them saying to Joe long time no see. Joe smiled then said how have you been this is Rose Brain said hello Rose welcome to our ranch Kendall said thank you. Brain said lunch should be ready soon, as they walked by he was checking out Rose from the back. Until he saw in the small of her back behind her belt a gun Don came out to introduce his wife ti them. This IS Joe Sandaro this this young lady is Rose Kendall greeted her in Spanish Maria smiled as they spoke to each other in her native tongue.

Don said after lunch lets talk business I would like to be filled in on what is going down. During lunch Maria along with her daughters talking to Kendall in Spanish, they got excited she had a identical twins. Don ask Joe does her twin knows what she is up to? Joe said you heard two heads are better then one. Don looked surprised then said two Black Rose's Joe said Only the family knows that.

Don's daughter's Susan and Peggy ask Rose to go riding Kendall said sure but first I need to discuss business with your father. After lunch Joe,Don and Kendall went to the patio in back Don ask her what do you have planned? Kendall taking out the picture of the house then saying this is his house. This large hill here over looking the land and house is prefect, if I can get a hand glider I can set it up on top of the hill take him out using the glider to get away. Don said clever I know some one who has a hand glider you can land it in my pasture. Tomorrow we can take a helicopter ride so you can see what you are dealing with. Kendall ask do you know if there is outside lights? Don said no it does not it was built fifty years ago and no pets.

Kendall said great Don said so relax from your flight today see Burton burnt down my uncle business in New York many years ago. I think my daughter are waiting for you Kendall got up ad headed to her waiting group. Brain came down and joined his father and Joe Don saw the gun on Rose looking at Joe he said she is carrying! Joe said that is not all she has on her. Brain said that is not right so beautiful and so deadly Joe said Burton made a mistake and thought he killed her. Don said what! Joe went into the story telling him everything as they watched her get on the horse.

Around and hour and a half later the girls came back Kendall got off her horse Susan and Peggy went to put the horses up. Kendall was looking over the pasture Don,Brain and Joe was watching from the patio. Brain said here comes Ted Joe said you better warn him! Don smiled I want to see how she handling him. He is a ladies man they saw Ted walk over next thing he was flying through the air. Landing on his back with a knife to his throat Brain said wow that was fast! Kendall looked at him in the eyes saying I am not your whore I suggest you back off. Don said now we need to go save my foreman the three walked over Don asking Rose to let Ted up, then asking what was going on ? Rose said he is getting to fresh.

Don said this is Rose our guest for a few days she also goes by another name the Black Rose Ted gazed at her then apologized. Later that evening the hand glider was delivered

Kendall would have to put it together. Ray went to tell Don the hand glider was delivered Don said thank you then asking would you be able to help her put it together when the time comes? Ray ask who is going to use it? Don said see that young lady with my daughters? Ray said her! Don said yes she is here on business. The next day shortly before lunch Don took Joe and Rose for that helicopter ride so she could see what she was dealing with. The hill was bigger then the picture which was good and the grass was taller.

Kendall ask Don if he could go from here to his ranch so she could get and idea how to go. By the time they landed she had everything down then she had to lesson to the news. Don said it is suppose to storm tomorrow afternoon Kendall smiled saying prefect. Don said excuse me! Kendall said what better way to mess up things then a nice rain. I want to leave four in the morning this way I can get set up and ready for him.

After lunch Don called Ray to tell him Ray said she is going to get up before the chickens. Don laughed Ray went on to say isn't it suppose to rain tomorrow? Don said she is counting on it Rose is going to try and get back before it hits. Ray said she is taking a chance Don said yes she is Tony Burton's mistake.

Four in the morning came Kendall dressed in all camouflage clothes to match the grass better. Joe pulled out a spray bottle saying hold up I want to spray you down with this .Kendall looked at it deer pee she said you want me to smell like deer pee! Joe said it will cover your sent in case they can get the dogs. Ray showed up with a pick up they loaded up and left, Joe went back to bed. They got as close as possible to the hill carrying up the hand glider they had it together in no time. Ray said good luck the left her rifle was across her back using the moon light she went down to the house. finding a table outside there on the patio then laying a black Rose on it the hurried back.

Hours later ten in the morning Doug walked out in the back yard near the edge of the cliff. Kendall took aim he turn his back towards her she shot hitting him between the shoulders he then fell over the cliff. Putting her rifle across her back and picking up the casing running down low hitching her self to the glider and she was off. Ten minute went by before his wife went looking for him going to the looking she looked down. She saw him laying down there on the ground.

She started to go inside to call the police when she saw the black Rose on the patio table screaming no. she called the police Don had turned on the police scanner he heard attention all units someone fell off the cliff then giving the address. Joe, Don and Ray went outside to keep a watch out for her a short time later they saw her coming in.

They ran out to meet her when she stopped she notice she was three feet away from cow poop. Some ranch hand went to help out she handed Joe her rifle so she could get out of the harness. As Ray and the ranch hands was taking apart the hand glider one ranch hand said nice rifle Rose said thank you it was a birthday present Rose ask need some help with that? Ray said no we got it Kendall said if you gentlemen do not mind I am going to go shower Joe spray me down with deer pee. Don laughed if they bring out the dogs that will mess thing up Kendall came out in a dress with her hair down.

A couple of ranch hands said wow she is pretty! Ted walked up to them saying watch your step around her I caught you two looking. She might be beautiful but she is very deadly I found out the hard way mean while Kendra was in Paris with her contacts. The got everything she ask for they also introduced her to and anointment that was deadly. They said in French it touches the skin it will cause death which looks like a heart attack. Her two contacts one was a taxi driver the other owned a funeral parlor with a section for cremation. Baptiste was the taxi driver the other name was Gabin he owned the funeral home.

Kendra speaking French ask do anyone have rubber gloves? Gabin said yes I do. Kendra then put the rubber gloves on first then a pair of black glove over them. Baptiste took her to the area where Charlotte was last seen so Kendall and her cousin Angel went shopping. Then day before she left she saw Charlotte Kendra set up for Charlotte to bump into her. Both women's stuff fell to the ground Kendra work fast to put her hand inside her purse. Dipping her finger in the anointment then grabbing a black Rose placing it in Charlotte's bag, while rubbing the stuff on the underside of Charlotte's purse strap. Angel and Baptiste acted like by standers helping to pick things up Kendra ask in French are you OK? Charlotte said did not speak French.

Baptiste said she ask if you was OK Charlotte said tell her yes and I apologize. Kendra handed her, her purse then everyone moved on Baptiste opened the door for Kendra and Angel then the taxi moved on. Kendra ask Gabin please take me somewhere where I can get rid of this stuff. Gabin said do not worry I will burn it up Charlotte was wearing a sleeveless shirt one of the purse straps fell to her bare arm.

The poison touching her skin she walked in the shop went to pay for what she picked out. Then falling down and died they called the police while Kendra and Angel went to Gabin's place to burn all the evidence. The gloves, the second bag and the anointment nothing

Black Rose

remind hooking anyone to Charlotte. Returning to their hotel with the thing they had bought there flight was for ten in the morning.

They examined Charlotte everything pointed that she had a heart attack. Kendra was in the air on her way home when the proper Authorities notified Lisa Burton Tony's wife about her daughter died of a heart attack. Her sister Valerie was with her Lisa made arrangements to have her shipped home Then passed out in shock all her children was now dead.

Joe meet Kendra at the airport grabbing her bags he said come on your sister is driving us nuts. He stopped at the store first and said Kendall is being a bitch no sooner did he stop. Kendall jumped out and ran inside Kendall ran around the counter to her sister giving each other a big hug. Charlotte's body finally arrived at home with all her belonging Valarie went to look in Charlotte's bag the one she used as a purse.

She saw something in the bottom the said to Lisa I do not think Charlotte died of a heart attack. Lisa ask what do you mean? Valerie reached inside pulling out a black rose. Lisa had a nervous break down ED Burton Tony's brother went to go visit him in prison to tell him the news. Tony said Charlotte was healthy and young Ed said Valerie found something to state there was interference. Tony ask what do you mean? Ed said there was a black rose in Charlotte's bag. This was a kick in the gut for Tony after several minutes of silence he said get me out of here! You here me and who is this black rose? Ed said no body knows.

CHAPTER 8

Upon graduation Curtis promised new cars to both Kendall and Kendra. so Connie,Curtis and the twins went to a car lot the girls went looking around for a car they like. Then asking the salesman if he had another car just like this one he said yes we do then went to go get Curtis he said a car is a car. Kendra and Kendall gave him a weird look Curtis went on to say girls it is OK to be different from each other.

Both girls gave him a look like he just insulted them then the salesman came up with another just like the one they had in mind. The girls looked it over then smiled at there grandfather Curtis paid for both of them. This girls got in the cars and raced each other home as they was pulling out Connie said to Curtis, they will race each other home then take one car when they go out.

A couple months passed when a French man name Antoine Caron paid a truck driver to deliver some merchandise for him. But the truck driver was in and accident the translator told him about the accident. Antoine ask now how do I move it? One of his employees said to him. Mr. Caron there is a smuggling ring around here to find it go to the

Black Rose

BBQ pit ask for Rose. Antoine thanked him not wasting time he went there the hostess ask a table for one sir? Antoine ask for rose in French.

The hostess called Kendra, Kendra ask whats up? The hostess said I do not understand this guy. I think it might be French Kendra ask est-ce que tu parles francais? Antoine said yes in French. Kendra ask how can we help you? Antoine said madam Rose Kendra said to Holly please ask my mother to cover for me and tell her about the gentleman. Looking at Antoine and asking him to follow her she took him upstairs then ask him if he will be eating? Antoine said yes. She translated the menu for him just when a waitress came up after she took his order. Kendra ask him why he was here? Antoine told her what happened and he needed some stuff moved.

Kendra said to him if you need anything moved go to this small airport then ask for Joe Sandaro. He can move it for a fee she wrote down the address then gave it to him then ask him to take and interpreter with him. She thanked him then minutes later his meal came she said bon appetit then left him. Antoine after eating went to pick up a person that could translate for him. Then going to the address given him Joe had two boys both teenagers and training to be pilots. They enjoyed helping out around the hanger there names Kevin and Porter he was the youngest. The two strangers walked up to Kevin asking for Joe Joe was doing some maintenance to one of his planes.

Now he owned three Kevin said dad some guys are here for you. Joe looked saying hello gentlemen how can I help you? The interpreter said my name is Marty I am here with MR. Antoine Caron who does not speak English only French. Joe said tell him I said good afternoon Antoine returned the greeting. Then ask something about the planes Joe said just making sure they run good. Then Antoine told him what he needed Joe said I can deliver it here is my price Antoine agreed to it and had the stuff deliver the next day.

Then Joe took it to the coordinates given to him latitude and longitude. Antoine told him to radio down before landing Joe saw the small airport off in the distance. Radioing down for permission to land a voice came back is this Mr. Caron's delivery? Joe said yes the voice said come on in. from the air Joe saw four police cars heading to that airport he radio down told them. That radio said hey the police are coming a worker ask who said that? The radio this pilot turning back to Joe the radio man said we was not aware of that sir. I want to give you knew coordinates go there you will contact Randy I will call ahead.

Joe put the numbers in and flew off thinking he could have been arrested. He saw the home made airport and radioed in this time he got a welcoming voice. Upon landing Randy came out to meet Joe asking if he was Joe Sandaro? Joe said yes sir. Randy then ask about Mr. Caron delivery opening a door saying right here sir Randy check it out. Smiling then saying to Joe thanks to you the police never found anything. Pulling out a very thick envelope handing it to Joe saying thanks for the heads up here is your payment and a little extra.

After police raid one of the worker there report what happen to Antoine Caron, Antoine said someone tip off the police. Find the informant and let me know mean while Joe made it back in more peaceful terms. A month past when Mr. Caron received a phone call telling him who the snitch was. Antoine got thinking this black rose has a nice touch then wonder if that young lady who spoke french would know how to find this black rose.

So Antoine went back to the BBQ pit Holly was setting people, when she saw the french man again saying to Kendra look who is at the door. Kendra look saying oh I got him then asking another waitress to cover for her. Looks like business then walking up to him and saying MR. Caron can I help you in french. Antoine ask can we talk? Kendra said yes follow me taking menu on the way up.

Taking him upstairs they both sat down Kendra asking how can I help you? Antoine ask do you know this black rose? Kendra said yes I do MR. Caron. Antoine ask is this person for hire? I like their style see I have a snitch in my company and this person almost got that pilot you told me about arrested. That got Kendra's attention she said the black rose will accept your offer. Antoine offered a nice amount of money to silence this snitch he then gave her everything he had on this person. When Antoine left she called the store Jake answered Sandaro General store. Kendra ask is Kendall there Jake hey Kendall

Black Rose

it is your other half Kendall said hey what is up? Kendra said we have homework. Then they hung up when they got home one called their uncle Joe for a plane while Kendra filled her sister in.

The other called this town and book a hotel for a week where this person lived at. Soon they was on there way the three of them was booked at this hotel, it took a couple days to find the target. They found the right spot then took him out with there marshal arts then laid a black rose on him. They finish the week sight seeing before they went home, the next day they was back Antoine's wife ask him to stop at Sandaro's General store and pick up a few things for her.

Antoine said I need to see someone then gave her a kiss before he left. Before going to pay Kendra he decided to stop at the store first he went in looking for what his wife ask for. He saw Kendall then he stopped he got thinking Kendra is working two jobs.

He walked up to her and said excuse me Miss. Kendra you work two jobs. Kendall look at him she knew he was french she said excuse me sir Antoine said you work two jobs here and the BBQ pit. Kendall smiled then said no sir that is my twin sister Antoine said twin! Kendall said you must be Mr. Caron. Antone said yes Kendall said we did a job for you Antoine took out a fat envelope then handed it to her. You have saved me a trip she then help him find the list for his wife when he left. Kendall called the BBQ pit Rachel answered BBQ pit Kendall ask is Kendra busy? Rachel said at the present yes. Kendall would you tell her Mr. Caron was at the store Rachel said sure thing then they hung up.

Kendra went by her to put and order up Rachel passed along the message Kendra smiled saying thank you. Rachel had a puzzled look o her face Connie walked up asking what is wrong? Rachel told her about the message From Kendall to Kendra. I think I missed something Connie giggled then said as long as you have known the girls and you are trying to figure there talk out, Rachel shook her head saying I don't want twins nope.

Some months passed there was a lawyer that was indictments was going down on. He worked for a mob family the head of the family was wanting him silenced, so he began to ask around and the black rose's name came up. He began to ask around again and a person said all kinds of people passed through the BBQ pit.

It is connected to a smuggling ring the man said thank you looking at his top man, he said I want you to go to this BBQ pit. You will need to ask for rose try and find this black rose I like this person's style. On one other thing I was told finding the black rose can be deceptive and looks are not what they appear.

Quinton ask what is that suppose to mean? The boss Luke Bishop I do not know but I know you should approach with caution. This black rose's nickname is the ghost Quinton ask does anyone knows what this person looks like? Luke said no that is why I want them. Quinton arrived in the area then checked into a motel, then asking the front desk where the BBQ pit was. The person at the desk gave him the direction and said the food is very good. Quinton said thank you then wanted to rest from the long drive.

The next day Quinton went to this restaurant, Holly greeted him asking a table for one sir. Quinton said I would like to speak to rose Holly took him upstairs setting him on the opposite side of the room. To where Connie and Douglas Miller was having lunch Holly handed him a menu then said someone will be right with you.

Then going down and getting Kendra and telling her your mother is busy and there is a gentleman upstairs. Kendra ask Sally can you cover for me business upstairs Sally said sure go ahead. Holly took her to the man Kendra ask him how can I help you sir? Quinton looked at her she appeared to be around nineteen. As she was setting down Quinton said I am looking for the black rose Kendra said I know a contact to the black rose. Douglas said to Connie that man there is Quinton Stevens he is known to be pushy, does not take no for and answer.

The talk between them was going know where Kendra was getting tired of it, she said sense your not saying why your looking for the black rose I am gone. Quinton grabbed her hand as she was getting up saying I am not done. Kendra pulled out her knife placing it on his wrist saying remove your hand or I will give it back to you. Quinton tried for the knife Kendra used her marshal arts knocking him out of

Black Rose

his chair. The move was fast then placing the knife to his throat she said do you think the black rose is going to say here I am! Now you better start talking your one step away from a coffin. Now Kendra and Kendall had engraved on their knives blades a rose.

Douglas got laughing at the site then said to Connie you should have seem your father in law back in his younger days. Quinton said alright please take the knife away as she did she held the side that had the rose on it to his eyes. Both sat back up to the table Quinton said you have some good moves. Kendra said I am a black belt Quinton said my employer is in need of the black rose's service. See there is a lawyer that has been indicted my employer does not want him to make it to court.

Kendra said I can pass what ever information on to the black rose's contact. Quinton pulled out some paper opening then to show a picture of this lawyer, then everything on him he then pointed to a phone number. This is my employer in new York inside Kendra was smiling the home Of Tony Burton, Quinton said my employers name is Luke bishop.

Connie's lunch date was done minutes Before Kendra's meeting was done. Kendra took all the paper work on this lawyer then said I will make sure the connection to the black rose gets this. Then getting up and leaving Quinton was setting enjoying his coffee after his meal. When Douglas walked up asking to set down Quinton said sure after setting down Douglas said the young lady you was talking to is Tony Burton's mistake. Then he told him the story Quinton said the news never said anything about a young girl. Douglas said that was to protect her she barely survived his beating and had to have surgery on her eyes so she can see.

Quinton ask does she really have a connection to the ghost or black rose? Douglas said one is the same in her grandfather's business, they have a lot of connections. When Kendra got down stairs Connie called her to the kitchen asking her what was that all about? So Kendra explained it to her. Connie said so he is looking for the black rose Why? Kendra said to kill this guy showing her the picture. A cook ask to see it so she showed him. He said it is the lawyer on TV three indictments word has it he has mob connections.

Kendra said he is in New York and has a contract on him the black rose was ask to do it. The cook New York you have family up there Connie we do! The cook smiled then said Sandaro's is bigger then you think. Kendra we will have to get a hotel the cook said let me make a phone call then he smiled. By the end of there shift that cook got Connie and Kendra together telling them they have a place to stay and they do not need a hotel. They said they have not seen the twins sense they were seven Connie ask where have they been? The cook said they was in a couple years ago. Kendra said we was out of town then this is going to be exciting.

That evening when dishes was done the twins called Joe asking him if he could take them to New York. Quinton waking up in the morning then headed back to New York after his break in Tennessee. While driving he got thinking of that young lady that took him down with a knife at his throat. She held it in front of his eyes he realized there was and engraving on the blade. Thinking hard what was it? It hit him a rose he came close on wrecking his car discovering she was the black rose. It came to him what he was told about deception is part of the black rose and looks are not what they seem. He got mad at his self he slipped up and it almost cost him his life he did not listen.

Joe said he would take them as busy has he has been he need a little vacation. Two days later they was off Joe could not wait to see his cousin's up on landing they was there waiting, they could not get over how big the twins got. A couple of the boys said to the twins you two are beautiful they twins said thank you Joe said hey they are family. Quinton had just got back reporting to Luke Bishop Luke ask how did it go? Quinton said the black rose. Luke ask how did you get the mark on our face? Quinton said I thought someone was toying with me. So I got a little demanding which almost cost me my life I did not pay attention to the story's on the black rose.

After Joe and the girls got settled in one of the twins called the number. Luke picked up the phone saying hello Kendall ask is a MR. Luke Bishop there? Luke said this is him. Kendall said this is the

Black Rose

black rose I here you have a job for me just wanted to let you know I am in town. Kendall said yes but I wish to ask something of you? Luke ask what would that be? Kendall said I wanted two members of the Burton's organization. Luke ask what for? Kendall said I want to pay my respects and I will contact when the job is done or you will here it on TV.

While Kendall was on the phone Kendra was asking her cousins where the address was. They enjoyed the rest of the day with there cousins the next day one of the male cousins took them to all this lawyers places he went. They even spotted there target he went down this small ally to get to another building.

The twins looked at thee watches for the time he was there the ally gave them and idea how to take him out. Borrowing the car the next day they went to the ally looking it over it was perfect for and ambush they went looking around until it was time. They went back fifteen minute before he was suppose to be there minutes passed then he came down the darkest part of the ally. They attacked killing him fast then setting him up against a wall with a black rose in his hand. It was hours later when a homeless man was cutting through the ally and discovered the body, he had just enough money for a pay phone to call the police.

Luke and Quinton was in there homes watching late night news when they told about finding the body of a lawyer And in his hand was a black rose. This got Luke's attention eleven o'clock the next day Kendall called Luke ask him if he was watching the news? Luke said yes I was I will have Quinton meet you at this park with your package. Then gave her a time their cousins knew the park Kendra went here to meet Quinton for her payment, along with information on the Burton's.

It was two men that worked for Burton's one enjoyed walking this trail through the woods. The other a rug dealer each twins took one Kendra took the hiker Kendall the drug dealer. A cousin took her to the trail Kendra was wearing a jogging suit and doing some stretches when the man showed up. Kendra had a fanny pack on with a black rose in it she followed him for some distance.

One part of the trial had a bend in it she rushed forward using her marshal art to kill him then laying a black rose on him. Kendall found her target setting in a car she pretended to be lost so she cold get close to him. She ask for directions reaching behind her pulling out her 38 automatic with a silencer then saying the black rose says hello shooting him twice.

Dropping a black rose on his lap then walking away his buyer found him twenty minutes later. Both girls meet back at the house happy they was successful on all there jobs. The spent the rest of the day relaxing with their cousins but the law still had no idea who this black rose was.

The money Kendra and Kendall earned through the black rose was laundered through the store and restaurant. When they got back home they got talking about a vacation so they could relax the contract was split in half then deposited. Kendra and Kendall drove to New Orleans for a week now Kendra was dating a man named Rusty Mitchell for few months. The girls went to a shop before they went to have lunch Kendra was on one side of the aisle Kendall on the other side it was short enough the could see each other.

There came in brothers to look around Mitch and Chuck Weatherly, now Mitch was not paying attention where he was going he was busy talking to Chuck. Mitch ran right into Kendall knocking her glasses off Mitch felt bad and apologized over and over. Kendall said watch where you are going next time and where are my glasses I hope you did not break them.

Mitch looked around and found them picking them up and handing them to her saying they are not broke. Kendall said thank you as she put them back on Kendra was looking at Kendall while Mitch was asking her if she was OK. Kendall said maybe you need glasses Mitch said like I said I am sorry I was not watching.

Kendall said I see Mitch said I was talking to my brother here allow me to buy you lunch. Kendall looked across to her sister saying I have a sister Mitch I will both of you lunch. Kendra nodded her head who would not turned down a free lunch. Kendall said you have a

Black Rose

deal Mitch said this is my brother Chuck walking around the aisle to join her sister Kendall.

Chuck said whoa twins both men looked at them they were identical if it was not for the glasses. Mitch ask where they wanted to go for lunch? Both girls mentioned the same place right down the road known for it's spicy food. How the girls talked caught both men off guard Kendra and Kendall paid for what they picked out then off to lunch. The hostess gave them a table for four both men pulled the chairs out for the girls. While they was eating Chuck ask if they had boyfriends? Kendra said I do she does not Kendall gave her a look like shut up. They talked through lunch then went sight seeing together before the split up Mitch managed to get a phone number. To where he could call Kendall the girls enjoyed their vacation in New Orleans soon it was time to go back home back to Tennessee.

Mitch had told Kendall he worked in law enforcement but never said how. A couple weeks went by and no call from Mitch he got wrapped up in a case his team was working on and forgot. They found the person they was after his team was six people so they took two cars, so they began driving where the person of interest was at.

While driving he saw a sign saying Sandaro's General store, all of a sudden Mitch said oh shit I forgot. Someone in the car ask what did you forget? Mitch told them about Kendall. Then said she is in that store just ahead I am pulling in I am going to go in and look for her. The rest of the team agreed the had to see how much trouble he was in. this time of day the store was slow she was stocking a few items when she heard a voice. Curtis was watching her turn her head she saw Mitch surprised to see him. She was trying to think of his name then said Mitch as if not sure Mitch said yes we meet in New Orleans Kendall said oh yes.

Curtis ask the others can I help you? Megan said no sir we are with him we want to see how much trouble he is in. Kendall you said you would call Mitch said I am sorry I got busy with work. Kendall ask what are you doing here? Mitch said we are passing through. Kendall said we! Mitch said come I will introduce you to my team. Kendall saw five people Mitch said this is Chuck, Adam, Julie, Megan and your boss Don. Guys this is Kendall we ran into each other in New Orleans Kendall said who ran into you knock off my glasses. Julie said this is getting good Kendall said the Grey hair man there is my grandpa this is my aunt Gwen and my uncle Jake.

They all said hello to each other Adam ask what do you mean who ran into who? Kendall I was looking at something when this big oaf ran right into me knocking my glasses off. Mitch said I did not break them Kendall said I am glad you did not I would not be able to see.

Don said you can not see without your glasses what is wrong with your eyes? Kendall said when I was around eight I have to have surgery on my eyes so I would not go blind. Curtis ask where are you heading? Don told him it has to do with a case we are on. Curtis said you will go by a restaurant called the BBQ pit if your hungry, before they left Mitch said when we are done with this case I will come back. Kendall ask are you sure you will not forget? So they left a week past before they was able to capture there suspect. Then they went home on the way back they stopped at the BBQ pit.

Kendra had been off and hour when they came in to eat she went home to relax. Around lunch time the next day Mitch called Kendall no answer so he went to visit his parents. Staying for a couple hours he called again no answer he had no idea she was working. He left for the store getting thee and looking around Gwen ask may I help you? Mitch said I was looking for Kendall. Gwen said she got off and hour ago Mitch looked disappointed Mitch said I called earlier and no answer Gwen said that is because her and her mother work.

Mitch ask may I use your phone? He called her number again Kendra answer it saying hello Mitch said Kendall Kendra smiled saying yes. Mitch said I have been trying to get a hold of you Kendra said sorry I was working. Mitch ask wold you like to go out for dinner? Connie walked by her at that time, Kendra said mom it is that dude Mitch that wants to date Kendall.

Connie said have him com over for dinner Kendra said Kendall will shoot you. Kendra said to Mitch how about come over for dinner mom has to meet you first. Mitch said I am calling from the store. just then Kendall walks in the room. Asking her mother who Kendra was talking to? Who was giving instruction on how to get here.

    Kendra hung up then said that was Mitch he is coming over for dinner Kendall said what! Mitch told Gwen thank you then left smiling. Connie said I want to meet him before you start dating him Kendall ask why? Connie said Kendra did not date Rusty until I meet him then same stands for you. Kendall said I just took off my make up Connie said you do not need it.

    Upon meeting Connie and seeing the twins together Connie ask him not to say anything about them. Because tony Burton killed my husband that is why he is in prison after this Mitch and Kendall dated up a storm. They got into ball room dancing along with Rusty and Kendra two years went by when one night during the news it said Crime boss Tony Burton had escaped from prison, the whole Sandaro family froze in shock to hear this.

CHAPTER 9

From the store the next day Curtis called his business partners they heard the news as well. They agreed to reestablish that contract on Burton for one million dollar to any hit they figure that should keep his head down. Then one day the lights came back on after years of being empty Tony Burton sat in his chair. asking his men who is this black rose? Tony was surrounded by his men. They said no one knows not even the law another man said no one is talking they all said they do not want there family to get a black rose.

Don called the team together in the conference room Adam,Megan,Chuck, Julie and Mitch everyone was all in place. Chuck said New York is keeping their eyes and ears open up there they are ready. Adam said his men played a part in his escape he has been running things even though he was a prisoner. Julie said a man like him and his wealth has more then one house Megan said we know he went to prison for killing Richard Sandaro. Don ask Mitch what is your girlfriends last name Mitch Richard Sandaro was her father. She was also in the car when Burton killed him he almost beat her to death.

Black Rose

Don what do you know about her family? Mitch said they are a very tight family you mess with one you have all of them after you. They are some things they do not talked about and Richard is one of them until her whole family is very nice. Don said we have our work cut out for us we need to find Burton he might try out your girlfriend.

Back at the house one of his men said MR. Burton we was asking and informant about the black rose. Well this one person we was pressing all of a sudden this person came buy and killed our guy. Then laid a black rose on him the informant as never said anything sense. While the employees at the BBQ pit which was mainly family and friends. Was talking about activity around the Burton house Kendra told Kendall they waited until eleven o'clock at night to go check it out. The road in front of the house had no street lights Kendall pulled over to the side of the road.

Kendra got the binoculars out and began looking in the windows. She spotted him telling Kendall then they left. They called Daisy the next day she was a cousin who paints ever sense she was ask to paint a scenic picture on a bare wall at the BBQ pit a couple years ago she had been busy.

Kendra and Kendall called Daisy asking her to paint a small picture. Daisy agreed so the twins bought her two arrows from a cross bow to Daisy she looked at them asking what is the picture? The twins said we want you to paint a black rose on these. Daisy said you got to be kidding me when you said small I did not think this small. you two are so lucky your family I will try and I will call you when I am done. The girls thanked her then left for work a couple days went by when the paint was dry Daisy took then to Kendall. Kendall looked them over and smile real big then ask how much they owed her.

The black rose was right under the feathers Kendall was so excite she called her mother asking her to tell Kendra Daisy finished them. Connie had not a clue what she was talking about but passed along the message. That evening after dinner the girls wiped the arrow clean of all fingers prints. That night at 10:30pm they left with their cross bow Connie got thinking that was odd and was wondering what they was up to. The twins said we find Burton we going to send him our regards the both smiled as they made there way to Burton's house.

They had dressed in black then covered the license plate right before they left for Burton's house. Pulling over on the dark street seeing and open window it was a hot night. Kendra was in the back seat with the window rolled down Kendall was driving. The curtains were open through the scope she found him taking aim Tony was setting in his chair she pulled the trigger. One of his men got up and walked across the room getting hit with the arrow instead of Tony the girls took off.

They saw he was hit with and arrow they worked the arrow out, one of the guys said what is this looks like a flower Tony looked then said or a black rose. Then looking out the window thinking that could have been him then giving orders to take him somewhere and bury him. Login Aaron got word about the contract then going to the BBQ pit setting at the counter. Connie comes from in back from the kitchen seeing Logan she walks over giving him a hug saying nice seeing you.

Kendra comes over placing and order then giving Logan a big hug as well. Saying Mr. Aaron nice to see you a regular customer went to tease Kendra saying Kendra when are we going out? Kendra smiled and said when hell freezes over. The man said your playing hard to get Kendra said if you do not behave I will tell your wife he laughed. Logan said in a low voice to Connie I heard about a contract! Connie said it is no rumor. Logan said he went under ground sense his escape Connie said would you like his address Login looked at her in surprise. Then said are you aware how many hit men that might bring that is a big pay day.

Connie said maybe he will keep his head down besides the black rose took a shot at him once already. Logan ask how did it go? Connie said the black rose used a cross bow as soon as the trigger was pulled someone stepped in the way. Logan said that has happened a time or two now Burton is going to be thinking the ghost is after him. Connie said ghost? Login said that is the name the underground has given the black rose.

Black Rose

Kendra came by to place another order Logan notice something then asking her if she was carrying? Kendra said a girl has to protect her self Login then said twenty twos! Kendra waited for the customer who was teasing her to take a drink of his coffee. Then said we have thirty eights Login and the man that was teasing her both burnt themselves on their coffee.

Connie got laughing the man that was teasing Kendra said you made me burn myself. Kendra said that is because you was thinking naughty thoughts I was talking about my gun. The customer said gun! Kendra said I have a family full of hunters and they thought my sister and I how to use them. So we could protect ourselves looking back at Login she said Sarah talks real Quiet.

Logan said you gave them names! Knowing what Kendra meant by talking quiet. Kendra said of course Kendall's is Susie Login said I forgot about your sense of humor. Mean while where Tony Burton was hiding out at the phone rang one of his men answered it after a brief conversation he hung up. Tony ask who was that? Troy the one that answered the phone said your brother Nick, he said there is a contract out on you for a million dollars. He has heard four hit men are trying for the prize money tony make that five this black rose or the other name the ghost.

Who ever it is, is clean but I did not have you guy bust me out of prison just to become a prisoner. Troy said Boss how many others will try for that prize you need to keep your head down you are a marked man. Tony ask who has that kind of money? Another one of his men said you do have some enemies.

Logan went back to his apartment he was renting he knew Tony Burton for he had hired him a few time to take out someone. Did he need the money? He had more then enough in his back account he knew Tony would be heavily guarded and by now know already about the contract. Then there are his students the twins Logan never trained anybody. Teaching these girls provided cover when he needed it along with it he like the girls. Spending all those years teaching them marshal arts how could he not like them. He then got thinking of Kendall there was times during class she would flip out and go psycho.

What Tony had done to her jumped in her mind now and then, it would take him and Kendra to snap her out of it. Once she was back she would set on the floor and cry he smiled knowing that she over came that obstacle, At sixteen the twins began making Tony Burton's life a living hell.

When the news came out that Tony Burton had escape prison all the Sandaro family began carrying guns again. This is one family you pick on one member you have them all on your back in this case they was protecting Kendra and Kendall. Tony Burton knew nothing about the twins and the family wanted to keep it that way.

Fours assassins came to town three men one woman they all got hotel rooms. the also did their homework on Burton they knew about the battle between him and the Sandaro family. They rested from their jet lag that day going out that evening for dinner they ask around the Sandaro family. Finding out they was a large family but also finding out about their store and restaurant.

Jamie the woman assassin figure to go to this store the next day, like the other three they had there dinner and look around. Very close to lunch time the next day Jamie pulled in the parking lot noticing a place to ear across the street. Walking in she saw Gwen at the counter and people looking around. When everyone left Jamie walked up to Gwen asking if she could help her find the Sandaro family? Gwen ask her why she was looking for them? Jamie ask I was hoping they could lead me to someone. Curtis had just walked up saying hello to Jamie Gwen said to her dad she is looking for someone.

Curtis ask who are you looking for? Jamie said Tony Burton I know he has escape from prison. Curtis ask do you work for him? Jamie said you could say I am a bounty hunter and there is a price on his head. Then Kendall came up she had been listening in Curtis wrote down the address giving it to Jamie. Saying he is here and heavily guarded Kendall said the black rose is after him also.

Jamie said oh Kendall said according to the rumors someone ruined that shot. Jamie ask how was that? Kendall said the person shot and arrow through and open window. Then someone stepped in the path of the arrow Jamie said what rotten lucky. Jamie said thank then turn to leave as soon as she touched the doorknob what Kendall said came to her mind Jamie was a stickler for details. Then she walked out thinking on how Kendall talked.

Gwen said dad did you see that she hesitated at the door Curtis said she might have been thinking on what Kendall said. Kendall said watch this reaching under the counter and pulling out a fake black rose. Gwen ask what is that doing under there? Kendall said with a smile when those teen boys come in running there mouth I put this out and they get real quiet.

Kendall made her way to the door looking out the window and watched, Curtis said to Gwen them two have a mean streak. Gwen said no daddy they don't take no shit from men Curtis laugh a little then said that is a good thing. Jamie was almost half was across the parking lot going to eat at that restaurant on the other side of the street. She stopped decided to go talk Kendall some more, as she turned she saw Kendall standing therein front of the store.

Jamie observed the way she was standing as one that did not take no bull. But what was in her hand? Jamie's eye went wide when she realized it was a black rose no her! Then a smile came on Kendall's face Jamie got wondering what did she walk into? Looking at Kendall in disbelief. Then slowly walking over to her Jamie said I am not after the Sandaro family I want the contract on Burton.

Kendall smiled Jamie ask would you like to have lunch? Kendall said just a minute. She went in the store putting away the fake rose then saying she invited me to lunch. As Jamie and Kendall walked to the restaurant across the street Jamie ask what do you know about Richard Sandaro? Kendall said he was my father then went on to tell her the story. Jamie said you survived and became a thorn in his side while this was going on another one of the hit men went to the BBQ pit. The hostess sat him down then the waitress came over to give him a menu. He said excuse me miss do you know how I can talk to someone from the Sandaro family? The waitress said 90 percent of the worker here is from that family.

The hit man said I am a bounty hunter and I am looking for and escaped convict Tony Burton. The waitress said that name will get you hurt here then walked away telling Connie about him she went over saying I was told you are looking for someone. She then sat down the hit man repeated what he told the waitress Connie said if your a bounty hunter I cannot help you. A few minutes later the waitress comes back asking are you ready to order sir? He placed his order the waitress left something told him there is more then meets the eye here.

Looking at Connie he said there is a wanted poster on him with a very big pay out I am after that. Connie smiled then said a million dollars does catch people interest the hit man said it sure does I want it. Connie said you and four others the hit man said four others! Connie said yes the black rose is one of them. The hit man said I see this is going to be a race who gets him first Connie slipped him a piece of paper saying here is where he is at, he does have body guards. Then she left well later that day at the end if there shift another ht man comes in Kendra had just clocked out and the hostess was busy.

Kendra ask may I help you? The hit man said I was told I could get information here. Kendra said so you need to talk private the hit man said if that is possible. Kendra ask will you be eating the hit man said yes Kendra grabbed a menu then said to the waitress at the counter tell Maggie she has one upstairs, then telling him to follow her.

Kendra sat him at a table for two then sat with him asking him when he was looking for? The hit man said I am looking for Tony Burton everyone knows he escaped. Kendra ask why the Sandaro's? The hit man said he went to prison for killing Richard Sandaro. Just then the waitress showed up ask if he was ready to order? He gave her his order then she left. He looked back at Kendra saying I also found out he was trying to take over their business. Burton is not the kind to give up Kendra said most of the people here are from the Sandaro family.

Some of them have to pass the house he owns to get here so yes he is being watched and the black rose showed there presents. Kendra wrote down the address to Tony Burton then gave it to him, the hit man said another assassin hmm Kendra said altogether there is five after him counting you.

His food was brought to him Kendra said enjoy your meal then left with the waitress. Once down stairs she ask the waitress Stella would you write something for me? Stella ask why what are you up to? Kendra said that gentleman upstairs is after Burton, I want to leave a note on his car from the black rose. Stella said in other words you want to mess with him Kendra said yes I gave him Burton's address I don't want him to match my hand writing. Stella said with a smile sure what do you want? Kendra said write good hunting the black rose.

Stella wrote it down then handed it to Kendra she said this is going to be fun to see his face. Kendra left placing the note under his wiper then got in her car and left. Stella had told a few other waitresses and they watched him as he left, but before he got in his car he saw the piece of paper under his wiper. Taking the paper he read it and was surprised who it was from the look on his face had some waitresses laughing as he looked around.

Each of these hit man was given Burton's address they spotted each other as they was casing out Burton's house. Then they agreed to meet at the BBQ pit second shift was in full wing. They had ask the hostess if they could have a private seating for four. The hostess said your lucky there are no reservation's pr parties going on upstairs. She took them upstairs then gave them there menu's. There name's were Jamie, Warden,Clay and Tyler Warden ask which one of us is the black rose? Tyler said it is not me I got a note from this person saying good hunting.

Jamie said it is none of us I accidentally crossed paths with the black rose. Clay ask as the waitress came back up to get thee orders who is this person? Jamie said I will not say this much I will say I was caught off guard. When I discovered this person standing a short distance behind me Tyler ask did this person say anything? Jamie said no they just held a black rose. Warden said that would give me a very bad feeling then the waitress brought thee food up. Jamie said it did I had to do some convincing I was after Burton not the Sandaro's this person relax.

Clay said another after the contract! Jamie said no the others looked at her. She said you heard me right for this person it's revenge when it comes to Burton's organization this person is as cold as ice. Clay ask where did this person come from? Jamie said from one of Burton's mistakes. Tyler said Tony has always been careful Jamie said Burton was trying to take over the Sandaro business around here and did something sloppy. He murdered Richard Sandaro but there was a second person in the car, A child he beat the child unconscious the left them for dead.

The child survived and has become the black rose this same person is collecting dirt on Burton's organization as much as they can. Warden said having someone on my trail that I don't know or can not see that would have me always looking over my shoulder. The waitress came back asking if everything was good they all said yes then the waitress ask if they would like dessert? On which all four ordered. After they had their dessert she brought theirs bills she also said I was ask to bring this note to this table.

This waitress place it in the middle of the table as she walked away Clay picked it up reading it out loud. It said Burton is getting itchy feet the black rose he said how does this person know we are here? Tyler said I found a note on my car. The four went down to pay there bills the twins were setting at the counter. Both wearing hats Kendall pulled her down to cover her face when Kendra said they are coming down stairs. both girls was giggling as the men paid and left Jamie spotted Kendall walked over to say hi. Jamie said hello Kendall Kendra said that is Kendall I am Kendra Kendall then raised her hat so Jamie could see her face.

Jamie was shocked to see twins both girls had a wicked grin on there faces, they said to her Burton knows about one of us not both. He also likes to set on his patio in the back yard where no one can see him. Jamie said I will tell the others the waitress came back asking the twins if they would like anything else? Kendall said yes cheese cake please. The waitress sad coming up Jamie said she ordered one the waitress said when it comes to these two they order the same thing.

Black Rose

There is nor difference on what they eat, drink or wear Jamie said I have meet twins before but nothing like you two.

Jamie said nice meeting you two then she left to find the men waiting for her in the parking lot. She filled them in on what the twins said Clay said I think we need to check this out. So they went to the address sure enough through the windows they could see him. Then a couple days later they saw this man with a beard and mustache, hat and glasses on. Two of the four hit man knew Burton it took then a few minutes until they realized who it was.

Then told the rest after the attempt on his life he had his men patrol the grounds. The four hit men saw a dark colored car pull to the side it was in the darkest part of the road around Burton's house. A person dressed in a black jumped out Jamie noticed the size of the person. Then smiled she said to the others boys meet the black rose Clay said where? Jamie said see the movement that person in black. The four watched as she stayed in the shadows Burton's patrol came around they saw her jump out and was amazed how fast she killed him.

They watched this person take something out and lay it on the body then leave. Warden said if that does not send a panic with Burton there is something wrong. Warden and Clay knew Burton he had hired them at one time or another to take someone out. Burton was wondering where Eddie was it should not take him this long he said to Marty and Steve go find out what is taking Eddie. Both men got there flash lights they found him laying on the ground Steve ask what is this? Shining the flashlight on the rose. Marty checked him then shook his head they took the rose and went inside.

They went back to Tony telling him we found him alright dead Tony stared at them asking how? Steve showed him the black rose. Tony's mind went racing who was this person toying with him then telling his men go bury him beside Nick. It was close to lunch the next day Tony Burton put on a disguise on saying he was wanting to go out one of his men said there is a restaurant called the BBQ pit that has some good food.

Tony smiled saying let's go four of his men went with him so they left surrounding Tony as they left the house. They got to the BBQ pit none followed Logan Aaron was already there he preferred this one table that was hidden it was how the lay out was. He could observe through a reflection Jamie sat on the other side to have lunch. Tony walked in with his men in disguise the hostess seated all five men together. After they ordered Kendra came out to check her section, Logan saw the mean look from that guy. Something about him his mannerism it hit him Tony Burton Kendra came by asking to refresh his coffee.

Logan said sure as she was pouring he said see this man in the reflection? Kendra ask you mean the one with the hateful look? Logan said yes that is Tony Burton. Kendra said he will think I am Kendall if he tries something Sarah will start talking. Logan said go about your business like normal tell your mother I would like to speak to her. Kendra went and told her mother Mr. Aaron was wanting to talk to her, then Kendra went to Amy asking her if table six was in her section. Amy said yes Kendra said that lady at that table is Jamie let her know that man at table eleven in the bread, hat and glasses is Burton.

Amy said he is not in my section but I will sing like a bird to her, Connie went to Logan asking what was up? Logan said the meal was very good. But there is someone here that interest me then he pointed out Tony Burton Connie looking at the reflection then said the fox came out of his den. He is going to think Kendra is Kendall that gives me and idea thank you one of the assassins is here eating. Connie went to leave for her table and saw Amy talking to Jamie smiling real big Jamie looked saying thank you.

She had just finished her meal paying for it and leaving a nice tip then went to her car. Connie and Kendra always had lunch in the office Connie ask did you see Burton here? Kendra said yes mama Aaron pointed him out. Connie said I have a plan now hear me out first. Burton and his men will be back they will think you are Kendall so I want you to go to the cabin. I will tell everyone here if anyone ask tell them you went on a vacation, Kendra ask do you think people

Black Rose

will ask where I am at? Connie said people no but Burton and his men might.

Now sense he saw you he will come after you Kendra said the assassins can get a better shot at him. Connie said that is right and I will have your sister call Megan Kendra said she is worried about Mitch Connie said I know I cannot ease her mind. Kendra said mom your doing the best you can Connie with hurt in her eyes said we need to kill him.

Kendra went back to work Connie called Joe, Joe ask what can I do for you, first how are things going? Connie Said Tony Burton was here with his men. The hatred in his eyes when he saw Kendra said everything I would like you to take her to the cabin in the morning. Joe said I have a job to do I will have Kevin take her Connie ask how is the food in the cabin? Joe said the freezer is full of game the rest should be OK I will buy some more just in case.

Connie said good I will call dad then they hung up Connie then called the store. Gwen answered how are you doing? Connie told her about Burton being there Gwen said I do not like that. Connie said he was giving Kendra a mean look then she told her about her plan. Gwen said dad just stocked the can goods a couple of days ago hmm hat plan might work I will stop by tonight.

Everything was set Connie prayed it would work Curtis had information on Tony Burton's organization on how to hurt it. Placing everything in a big envelope Gwen told him about Connie's phone call. Curtis listened to Connie's plan then said if her plan work he is dead just like my son pay back. Gwen said I am going to her house tonight Curtis went to his office opened his safe then pulled out a thick yellow envelope. Taking it to Gwen he said have Kendra take this to the cabin if Mitch's group helps give it to them. Gwen ask what is inside? Curtis said information on Burton's Organization.

Gwen went home cooked dinner for her husband and kids then left for Connie's after dishes. They all sat in the living room as Connie unfolded her plan to Gwen and Kendall, Kendall said ma ma your going to separate us! Connie said he was at the restaurant today. The look he gave Kendra was pure hate he will come after her both girl had tears in there eyes it was the separation this would be there first accept for the hit. Then you call Mitch's group get them in to it more tears came down Kendall's face.

Kendall said no mama he must stay out of this Kendra was feeling her sisters emotions. Connie said sweetie I understand believe me I do but he will want revenge. Kendra said the black rose got revenge Connie said Tony Burton tried to take more then he could handle, messing up big time I need both of you to stay strong bring out the black rose if you must.

In the morning both guns made sure the had their guns, Connie ask Kendra if she knew how to get into the gun room? Kendra said yes and I have the envelope that aunt Gwen gave to as well. Then Kendra boarded the plane at ten in the morning while in the air Kevin said you will not be alone up there, family will be camping out in tent all over up there. It was three days later some of Burton's men came in asking a waitress about Kendra. The waitress told them what Connie wanted them to know then she went and told Connie. She said thank you now if they take the bait Burton must die the waitress ask how are the twins doing? Connie said boy they are a handful.

After Burton's men ate they went and told him about Kendra also where she was vacationing and the only way up there was horse back. The Sandaro's had been keeping track of the four assassins and giving them updates on Tony Burton. Tony ask where is there a riding stables at? One of his men said I heard there is one eighteen miles east of here. Tony said lets go ride some horse's he did not know her was being watched, the assassins rode the way to the AA stables. They saw and abandon house half way there they would try and force him here. Out in the middle of no where Tony had eight of his men left a call to Kendra was made. When Kendall hung up Curtis saw the look in her eyes almost in tears on her next move.

CHAPTER 10

Very close to lunch time Kendall called Megan a lady that work in Mitch's groups her boyfriend. Megan answered hello Kendall said who she was Megan said Kendall how are you? Kendall ask can we meet for lunch? I have information on Tony Burton. Megan said sure where at? Kendall said the BBQ pit tell the hostess you want to speak to rose, Megan ask you not setting me up for the black rose are you? Kendall said no oh and exterminate your office understand. When hanging up Megan wrote down we are bugged then knocking on Don's door showing him the note while telling him she was going to lunch.

After Kendall hung up from Megan she called Samuel asking him to pick her up and take her to the restaurant. Samuel was a cousin he pick her up at her house she came out wearing a red wig a hat with sunglasses. When Sam dropped her off they both went in Sam sat at the counter while Kendall told the hostess she was expecting someone. Then walking back in the kitchen asking dog to put back a rack of ribs with sweet BBQ his real name was Lewis. He was her uncle he got that nick name in his late teens and it stuck with him.

Black Rose

Turning to leave and go upstairs Kendall ran into her mother she told her that Megan was on her way. Then stopping at the waitress at the counter telling her let Lucy know she has two people upstairs please. Then she headed up and picking a table across the room no more then ten minutes later Megan walked in. the Hostess said a table for one ma'am Megan said I am here to see Rose the hostess said follow me please taking her upstairs. Megan saw Kendall and went over to her and setting down the hostess telling Lucy her guest were here. After setting down Megan ask what is up? Kendall said we smoked out Tony Burton and we need your help.

Megan ask why did you not call Mitch? Kendall said I do not want him in on this. Megan said you have no choice he is on the team this raddled Kendall Megan could see it. Kendall said Burton is on his way to AA stables as we speak four assassins will try and force him in and abandon house. The waitress had already came up and took their order as Lucy brought there order Megan's cell phone rang. While Don told her they found the bug Lucy whispered to Kendall he is pinned down in that house four more of his men are dead. Kendall said thank you Megan filling Don in on what was said.

Don was very interested when it came to Tony Burton, as they ate Kendall told Megan what Lucy told her. Megan said they are after the contract Kendall said yes my family has made a plan. Megan ask what is it? Kendall said Burton thinks there in only one way to our cabin horse back. Because that is what we told his men when there are two ways Megan ask what is the other way? Kendall said and airplane it is the kind that lands on water. Megan said Don is very interested maybe you should tell your plan to him.

Lucy came back asking if they would like desert? Megan said no thank you Lucy then left the bills. Before she left Kendall ask her could you tell dog to get the ribs ready please that I ordered. Kendall put back her disguise before going down to pay her bill then nodding at Sam on the way out, both got in Megan's car. To go talk to her team a little light came on on Kendall's purse Kendall placed her finger to her lips saying shh. Moving her purse around until she found it. A listening device Kendall took it and put it under the car tire Megan looked at her asking where did you get that? Kendall smiled then said I have my source's you have yours.

Then they left for Megan's office Kendall came out of the wig and sunglasses. Megan said you have some remarkable contacts Kendall giggled she had placed that box of ribs in the back seat. They was half way there when Megan said those ribs are smelling up my car Kendall said tell your friends it is a car deodorizer. Megan ask what should we call it keep them hungry they both laugh they soon pulled in the parking lot then went in. Megan went to Don the rest of the office ask smells good? Mitch just came out of the bathroom and saw Kendall. Asking her what was she doing here? Kendall said Burton is on the move.

Kendall dug into her black rose side, Don call everyone into the conference room. As they took there seats Kendall sat the box of ribs in the middle of the table with a bag of napkins. Don said Megan says you have information on Tony Burton Kendall said he is on the move right now he is pinned down in and abandon house on straight creek road. One of the group ask where is he heading? Kendall said he is after my sister our family owns a cabin in the mountains and we let it leak she is on vacation up there.

We also made it clear there is one way up on horse back, he is heading towards the AA riding stables. There is really two ways up Don ask why bait him knowing how dangerous he is? Kendall said to draw him out for the assassins. One of the group said that is right that contract that is out on him Chuck said that smell is making me hungry Kendall said dig you all. Adam said we heard there are five assassin after him, Kendall said there is six one is working with my family. They all looked at her Don said you know he is a hit man? Kendall said yes Megan ask why? Kendall said he has worked with Burton on some occasions.

He knows Burton good and had turned against him Julie ask why? Kendall ask do you all know why he was in prison? It did not hit Mitch until after he said yes. He killed Richard Sandaro the same last name as yours Kendall said was a witness to the murder. A little girl she was eight after he killed my father the group froze on those words. Kendall went on he saw her then went over and tried to beat her to death. Then he did his best to blind her but I survived and I hate that man my family has set a trap we want your group to spring it.

They had been eating while Kendall was talking Don said to get Burton we will do it Kendall said here is the rest of the plan. Megan there is a small airport south of town Megan said I know of it. Kendall said you go there as for Joe Sandaro he is my uncle tell him you was invited to go fishing. The rest of you go to the AA riding stables ask for Ray tell him the same thing. He will give you a map for the short way to the cabin by the end of the meeting they was cleaning up.

Don ask when will we do this? Kendall tomorrow ten in the morning right now there is a gun fight taking place. Chuck said I think it is best we stay out of that fight Adam said let them kill each other. Don said Tony Burton has got himself out of more scrapes then you know that is why he is New York's worst crime boss. As Mitch's phone rang Don said ten bucks says Burton gets away from those assassins. Mitch answered it saying OK then hung up then said to Kendall that Sam was outside. Kendall said ladies and gentleman my ride is here I am on my way to join my sister.

Kendall got in the car as they pulled away Sam said someone was about to send a picture of the black rose doing a hit. We was able to find the person Kendall ask did you kill him? Sam said no but we got our point across. Arriving at the airport Joe was ready Sam took her bags to the plane, Kendall told Joe that Megan would be here tomorrow she will have her gun with her. Not wasting time they was off but for Kendall the plane was not going fast enough. Once it landed she could not get out of the plane fast enough running towards each other and giving each other a big hug.

Don ask Mitch how much of what she said do you know? Mitch said I did not know about the beating. The Sandaro's is a secretive family you pick on one you got all of them to deal with. Julie ask what is it with her and her sister? Mitch said Kendall's mother made me promise not to say anything about her sister. To protect them against Burton Adam said I am missing something here. What does Burton have to do with this? Mitch said at one time Burton and the

Sandaro's was at war. A power struggle Burton was wanting the store for smuggling.

Chuck said there is bad blood between the families Mitch said very bad blood, if we don't get Burton I promise you he will not leave that mountain alive. Don said let get him Kendall sound like she had a good plan, in the morning they followed her plan Megan went to the small airport. Asking for Joe Sandaro Kevin Joe's youngest greeted her telling her to follow me. He said dad someone is hear for you Joe ask how can I help you? Megan remembered what to say to him I was invited to go fishing, Joe said right this was ma'am we will take this plane.

Megan said that is the kind that lands on water! Joe smiled saying that is the only way up there. Joe said do not worry miss I have made this trip many times once in the air Joe said when you get up there you will see one of the biggest secrets in our family. Joe got on the radio calling silver eagle to crows nest a voice said go ahead silver eagle Joe said someone is coming up fish. The voice said Roger that silver chicken the twins got laughing Joe said I am going to get them for that. Flying for a bit Joe said see that lake? Megan said yes Joe said that is where we are going to be landing Megan looked at it saying your kidding.

The twins were waiting by the dock Joe said look as they pulled up Megan looked in surprise saying twins. She carefully got off the plane the twins ask their uncle if he would like to stay for some trout and mac and cheese. Joe said I need to get back then turned around and took off Megan just looked at them then ask who is Mitch's girl? They both giggled Kendall said I am.

On the way to the riding stables Mitch told the rest, they all piled in one van. That Kendall was helping him get over his fear of horses Julie said we did not know you had a fear of horse's. Mitch said it goes back to my child hood we had horses we also boarded horse's when I was nine I was thrown from a horse. Then when I was ten I was helping my dad clean out a horse barn piling the manure at one end for the tractor. A horse caught me off guard and kicked me sending me in the pile of manure, I spent three days in the hospital with fractured ribs.

They no sooner got at the stables Mitch put and apple in his pocket, Chuck ask who is that for? Mitch smiled saying my girlfriend. Adam said Kendall will kick your butt Mitch saw Ray calling him over telling him they been invited fishing. Ray looked at the group telling them to follow him, leading them a short distance away from people. Mitch leaned against the coral fence as Ray came back with two sheets of paper. Ray said you all just missed Burton he is on the two hour tail he has twenty minutes on you. Don ask how close to the cabin does he come? Ray said close enough to barely see it. Julie said as a horse nudged Mitch we need to beat him up there Mitch turned to look Ray said Savannah likes you.

Mitch reached in his pocket and pulled out the apple saying here you go girl. Ray is the sweetest horse we have then showing them a second paper asking Mitch do you remember this way up? Mitch said yes it comes up behind the house. Ray said yes the left side take them up that way Chuck ask you have been up there before? Mitch said a few times with Kendall. Ray said your horse's are being saddled as we speak Adam ask what about Mitch's girlfriend here? Ray smiled then said she is going to be ready in a few minutes she likes Mitch.

Julie teased Mitch cheating on Kendall with another girl Ray laughed saying this girl Kendall will not mind. Now Mitch when you get up there keep going until you see tents Don said tents! Ray said if you get killed in this he is fish food. We have three dozen people up there all of them are armed a stable worker whistled for Savannah. She went over to Brenda so she could put a bridle and saddle oh her she got excited. Brenda yelled hey Mitch come over here so she will settle down the team teased him as he climb over the fence.

Ray said to the rest you folks need to get him dead or alive you get him the law sees it case closed, we will protect our own Burton want revenge. As they all mounted up Mitch as everyone ready one by one they all said yes Mitch said OK lets move out follow me. Don ask you want this map? Mitch said no I got this the team could tell that Mitch had been up here a few times. Chuck ask what does this cabin look like? Mitch said it is beautiful and sets on the edge of a lake.

They rode for sometime when they saw the cabin they turned to the left, until they saw a lot of tents someone came out to meet Mitch and his team. Getting off the horse the people in the tents took the horses aside, now the twins had shown Megan where to hide at This is where they believed Burton would come. When Don and the rest got there a person ran and told the twins and Megan while a man filled in Don's team.

We have the trail he is coming on covered, we grew up around this cabin and hunt here. So this is like our back yard so if you all get shot or killed three dozen if us will finish this. Don said let hope it does not come to that just then a walkie talkie broke in saying he is just about there. One of Burton's men is riding asshole the man and Mitch got laughing. Adam ask what is so funny? The man said that is the name of the horse Julie said your kidding! You don't name a horse that.

The man said that horse has a nasty attitude it depends how he feels that day if he lets you ride him. Mitch said Kendall and her sister gave the horse that name Julie ask why? The man that talked with them said Kendall and her sister tried to ride him. He end up throwing both of them they got up at separate times calling him and asshole and a few other names. Both looked at the horse and said look asshole we are riding you just then a voice came over the walkie talkie he spotted the cabin.

The twins and Megan went to her hiding spot everyone one else got ready Don said come on team. They saw five horse's arrive on horse all black with a while mark between his ears. Reared back dumping his rider Don said let me guess asshole Mitch smiled saying yep sure is showing his personality. Burton and his men dismounted then helping then helping then one on the ground up. Tony said lets look this place over you four go around that way I will go this way so they split up Tony was almost in front.

When Kendra stepped out she said hello Tony longtime no see, she had Sarah in he belt at her lower back. Tony said I am going to kill you then Kendall stepped out asking or is it me? Tony was shocked

Black Rose

identical twins. Megan jumped out saying Tony Burton freeze your under arrest Tony raised his gun to shot Megan fired twice hitting him both times. Tony fell his men came running right into Don and the rest a gun fight took place Megan went to help. The twins looked down at Tony both bullet wounds were critical they said we are going to tell you who the black rose is before you die.

We are the black rose you killed our father we took your family he tried to say something then died. Kendra using her marshal arts hit him to make sure he was dead, the other gun fight did not last long Kendall hid. Don ask Megan where is Burton? Megan said I shot him he is over here the followed her. Kendra was standing by the body Adam ask Kendall are you OK? Kendra said I am not Kendall just then she stepped out saying I am Kendall. The team was stunned Kendra said Mitch your wounded Kendall went to get bandages.

Mitch said it is just a graze Kendra said if your team can get the bodies to the dock. we can call our uncle to fly up and get them out of here Mitch come with me and we will bandage you up. As Mitch sat there in a chair on the porch while the rest was moving the bodies.

Kendall handed Kendra the bandages the went to the radio saying silver eagle from the crows nest. Joe said go ahead crows nest Kendall said our guest caught some fish we need some bags so they can take them home. Joe said Roger that I am on my way up while patching up Mitch Kendra told Mitch that Kendall was scare to death for him. When Kendra was done Mitch went inside looking at Kendall he said we need to talk.

He then kissed her Kendall smiled saying I like this conversation they kissed again. Kendra smile Julie and Megan ask where is Mitch? Kendra giggled pointing in the house. Megan and Julie said excuse me! Mitch looked then said I am interrogating a witness. When Don and the rest was done they joined the rest Chuck ask where did Mitch go? Julie said in there repeating what Mitch said. They looked in Don ask when do we interrogated a witness like that? Mitch said she is about to talk.

Kendall said I need more interrogating everyone laughed Don called the law to have them meet Mitch at the airport. While the rest walked around to the horse's the twins saw him the both said asshole your here. Running over to him and giving him a hug the team said that poor horse having to live with that name. Two weeks went by Kendra and Kendall were in the barn with there guys radio was on. The was ball room dancing Mitch's team was there watching they had no idea he could do this.

Curtis and Cinder stopped by Connie said mom, dad come on in. Curtis ask where are the girls? Connie said out in the barn with there boyfriends. Cinder said in the barn with men! Connie said mom it is not like that they are dancing. So the three walked out to the barn when the door opened Kendra and Rusty just got done with the rumba. Mitch and Kendall walked out to do the quick step Kendra said grandpa grandma hello giving them both a hug.

Curtis ask what kind of dance are they doing? Kendra said the quick step Curtis said that looks fun. Kendra looked shock then said Grandpa your to old Connie said Kendra! Kendra said well mama they are. Curtis got laughing and said your grandmother and I use to been some find dancers in our day. Mitch and Kendall was done Kendall saw her grandparents rushed over and gave both a big hug. Kendra said they are going to dance Kendall look at her grandparents in shock then her mother. Connie said don't you even Cinder smiled and said to ?Curtis let show them how we did it, as they walked out they did the jitterbug.

www.ingramcontent.com/pod-product-compliance
Lightning Source LLC
LaVergne TN
LVHW091559060526
838200LV00036B/912